MINDING THE STORM

A YEAR OF STORIES

BY ELIZA LOEB

BLUE FORGE PRESS
Port Orchard, Washington

TABLE OF CONTENTS

MINDING THE STORM
A YEAR OF STORIES

BY ELIZA LOEB

Philia

Chapter 1

She sat atop the tower as night fell upon the horizon and cast its shadows throughout the city. Her thoughts roamed as they usually would this time of day and she hardly had anything clear to say about it. To some, she was your typical homeless millennial taking refuge under some bridge or another that no one likes to pay any sort of attention to. To others, those of the supernatural variety, she was a misplaced goddess of love. She knew her name, others only whispered it without realizing that she was even nearby. And like any goddess of love and beauty, she often grew angry at the sheer lack of knowledge that modern day humans had behind it.

"By the god's little sister, you look terrible," came a low, gruff voice.

Her golden eyes peered up from beneath a turquoise hoodie, all too aware of who had approached. His eyes were a steely blue, cold as death as they peered through the darkness as his dreadlocks had been pulled back into a ponytail, revealing handsome face with high cheekbones and dusky skin.

"So death has come to greet me in my darkest hour?" Hathor asked as she pulled her hood back. "Wouldn't you call that a bit cliché, Anubis?" She studied him closely, pursing her lips as he stood beside her in a suit with black and gray undertones, lightly accessorized with a single white scarf.

"I've come to take you home." Anubis answered. "The streets are no place for you."

"But what if I want to live on the streets?" she asked.

"Then Horus will come and take you by force."

Hathor roles her eyes and shifts as she makes a movement to stand. "When I said he and I were done, I meant it."

"But the gods marry—"

"The gods are flawed."

Her voice was full of agitation as she sighed and waved her elder brother away. Too long had she been revered by mortals looking for romantic love. Too long had she been perceived as the *wife* of Horus. And too long had she been used and mistreated for representing anything *but* lovers when her own marriage ended because she had no passion for a man who was supposedly the god of kings. And oh... did she hate being a side piece for him. And Anubis knew it.

"He can give you security."

Security? Is that what it was? Was this the damn eighteen hundreds where a woman gave herself to a wealthy man for the sake of security? Her brother was smarter than that. She was a deity who, despite her current disposition could and should be revered. Love had a very thin border with hate and is often in league with passion. To which, she had a lot of passion to go around.

"I can make my own security, brother."

"So you want to end up like the greeks?"

"The Greeks are still celebrated and live very comfortably."

"And their marriages are miserable."

"As was mine!"

Anubis took a step back, eyeing his younger sister for a brief moment before sighing in defeat. Hathor, had not realized that she had raised her voice. Yet now, there was a great deal of contempt for her brothers' visit. And with a single gust of wind, he dispersed into sand and left her alone.

Days passed, then weeks and Hathor never saw her brother. Rather, she stayed beside herself and wandered the streets, giving what she could to those who needed it most and only taking what was necessary for her. Eventually the winter came, and a key was dropped before her. She had given what she could, only taking what was necessary. Strangers on the street recognized her as a giver, referring to her as kind and loving and some whispered among themselves, asking why. She never gave them a name, she never told them to repay her or asked for anything in return, yet they still wondered.

"That kindness is gonna kill you, sweetheart," a man said to her one day. She shrugged it off, neither caring nor paying mind to his words.

Her gold eyes flickered beneath the street lamp as she leaned against the aluminum fence. The night air was cold and biting, with only a take away of soup to warm her hands. Seagulls could be heard, crying loudly to one and other in the distance. They were possibly scouring for food.

"Out here again?" asked an all too familiar voice.

Hathor looked up to find a taller man standing beside them. Long red hair draped over his shoulders as a hood cast a shadow over his face. She smiled in greeting, as if meeting an old friend for the first time in a while.

"You sound displeased." She laughed, looking out at city.

Seattle had been particularly lovely on quiet nights like these. If one had been close enough to the water, they could hear the sounds of the water splashing along the shore, brushing along the sands as if they were supposed to be whispering terrible secrets to the earth.

"Not with you, dear friend," the man said in response.

"But some of the humans I see in these parts."

Hathor's smile soon faded to that of a knowing look. The man standing near her had seen just as many horrors as she had. They had both seen the wars of their people, the fates of children left in the woods to die, the cruel hands of war and famine reaching into the deep crevices of the earth before inviting their companions death and pestilence to join in the tragedies.

"What happened?" she asked.

"Do you know of the term, A mother is god in the eyes of her child?"

Her eyes fixed on her friends face as she gently touched his shoulder. His face was twisted into a grimace as he looked away from her. He had seen something that disgusted him and she knew it. Often did he speak to her about his children, often had he beamed with pride as she asked. When they had gone to parks, he would take delight in watching the children play, encouraging their antics as they made up games or collaborated outlandish schemes to fuel their imaginations. And much without their knowing would throw in little illusions every now and again to help with the more whimsical aspects of their game.

"I know it well."

Her friend looks down at her with earnest as he slowly begins to open his mouth to say something, clamping it shut and gritting his teeth as he runs his hands through his hair, pushing back his hood.

"Today I saw a mother using her child as a crutch to get more money."

"You don't know that."

"But I do."

She sighed and gestured for him to continue, and he looked puzzled for a moment. As if to search for the correct words in a puzzle.

"Hatti, I see this woman every single day. I see her sitting at different street corners, I see her perching in different spaces of the city. I hear her child complain that they are hungry, pleading for food at night. I see people give her money and every single time she gets money, I stand and wait. Part of me hopes that this woman will come to her senses, while another part of me feels as though I am going insane for expecting a different result."

"Well, you do represent mental illness among other things…"

"Not helping, Hatti."

"Sorry."

The man turned and pressed his forehead against the fence, sighing in exasperation as he curled his fingers between the wires. There was a long silence that followed and Hathor found herself unsure of the situation. She questioned the situation, trying to find reason as to observe and make a judgement for herself. She had seen many children put in to the system by authorities, having been torn from a loving home for so much as a complaint regarding an inkling of neglect. She had seen families try and fail to fight the system and yet….

"Loki…" she pressed. "May I see this woman?"

Loki straightened himself and didn't bother to look at her this time. His expression was solemn, as though he was the father of the child in question.

"Yeah."

Chapter 2

Marcie Henderson *hated* taking the medicine. She hated the long grueling days of not knowing the difference between her left or right, and she hated not having friends or going to school.

"You have to *work* for your food," her mother had told her.

Often times, when she did work, she found that it would be for nothing. And when she did complain, she would either be stricken or threatened with death. The worse thing that came to mind, though, was something worse. She had seen older girls being traded off for *medicine*. *Medicine* was the stuff that all of the money went to, that their mother never bothered to see a doctor for. *Medicine* had many other names, more commonly known as crystal.

Marcie knew of other families in her situation. She would sometimes watch as they went to community gatherings to get a bite to eat, or safe places to spend the day while parents look for jobs to support themselves and their kids. Yet, she wouldn't dare bring her mother to those places. Those places often had rules. And rules were what separated children from single parents. And if that happened, who knew what would happen to her mother.

Her stomach twisted and growled, causing her insides to ache as hunger had begun to overtake her. She needed food, yet was unsure where to get any. She looked to the side to a cardboard mat where her mother slept. If the growling grew louder, she would surely be beaten. She slowly slipped out from beneath the sleeping bag they had gotten from a nearby day shelter, tiptoeing away from their sleeping area to try and scour for food and completely unaware of who might be following. She turned several corners and slipped in to a nearby 365 stop. She shivered as the warmth hit her, reveling in the sensation as her toes curled in the too big pair of tennis shoes she had yet to grow in to. She sighed with delight as she hugged herself, twisting and spinning in the warmth.

"Can I help you with something, little girl?" asked a feminine voice.

Marcie was pulled from her moment of warmth and blushed with embarrassment as she looked down. The woman who had been watching her had deeply tanned skin. Her hair had been pulled back in to a ponytail as bags had formed under her eyes and she looked to be no older than maybe her late twenties to early thirties. Likely someone who had been working a night shift.

"I was just trying to get warm ma'am."

"Don't you have a home to do that?"

It would be nice to have a home, she thought. She felt a heavy lump form in her throat as she looked around for an excuse as she slid her hands into her pockets. She didn't know how to answer the woman.

"Homes have rules."

The woman raised a brow with a puzzled expression as she crossed her arms. Was it something that Marcie had said? The woman craned her neck, trying to see if her mother had been nearby, and stepped out from behind the counter to step out the door for a brief moment. Her mother had been nowhere to be found. Once the woman had confirmed her suspicions, she moved her eyes back to Marcie, who now had a frightened look.

"Have you eaten?" she asked.

Marcie shook her head.

The woman sighed and pulled her behind the counter, pulling up a stool for her to sit. And like that, she was beginning to panic. Her thoughts were racing at nearly what seemed a million miles a minute and she couldn't stop them, and she began to cry. The woman looked back to her with a platter full of food and quickly set it aside to kneel before her and wipe her tears away. Marcie pushed her hands away and tried to wipe her tears away by herself. She tried to not be weak before a stranger. She tried to stop crying.

"Why are you crying?" The woman asked. "Did somebody hurt you?"

She shook her head and sniffled. Mucus had began to run from her nose, mixing in with her tears as she tried to calm herself down.

"I don't want to be taken away from my mom." Marcie pleaded.

"Well honey, by the looks of things, you're hungry and cold and she is nowhere to be found."

Marcie paused and looked up at the woman as if to ask what the woman meant. The woman simply held the platter of food before her, as though she hadn't said what she had.

"You don't have to finish it all, you just have to eat enough to stop the growling."

"But ma'am, I don't have any mon-"

"Don't worry about it."

"I don't even know your name."

"You can call me Hatti."

Hatti's golden eyes flickered in the light as she straightened and immediately, Marcie could see the movement of a familiar jacket at the corner of her eye. She paled, recognizing the rapid and jerked movements of her mother as she stormed in to the shop, looking around frantically and landing her eyes on Marcie, fixating them on her as she sneered.

"Are you stealing food now, ya little thief?" the woman hissed.

Thin legs began to stalk forward as Marcie backed into a corner. Her breathing became heavy as she knew what was going to come next. She cried out, babbling pleas and begging for forgiveness, afraid of what was to come, despite how futile they were. Loud shouting soon filled the shop as Hatti stepped between the two and pressed the woman back.

"She's a thief! She's manipulating you into feeling sorry for her so you can give her food!" her mother shrieked. Hatti looked back at her with a hard stare and then back to her mother as she lunged at Hatti, only to be shoved away.

"Get the fuck out of my shop," Hatti said coolly, pointing toward the door as she kept a firm barrier between the other woman and Marcie. The other woman narrowed her eyes at the little girl and Hatti stepped in her line of sight.

"Sweetheart, I suggest that you keep your eyes on me," the taller woman warned. "Because that little girl is not the one you're gonna deal with."

The smaller woman squared her shoulders as she did her best to match up to her new opponent, only to be shoved away again and stared down, making her way to the door.

Hatti flipped the sign as she crossed her arms, sneering as she watched Marcie's mother skitter away. Her attention moved back to Marcie and her expression softened.

"Are you hurt?"

Marcie shook her head.

"Good, because I am going to call child services."

Chapter 3

She sat inside the office, inhaling the smell of stale paint and printer ink for what seemed like a good while. She jerked at the slightest noise, in fear of being taken away by bad people as moment after moment passed. The kind lady could have also been one of the bad people. She did send her mother away and promised to protect her. Now her mother was nowhere to be found.

"Marcie?"

Marcie looked up to see Hatti smiling down at her.

"If you don't mind, you're going to be staying with me and a friend of mine for a little while."

"What about my mom?"

Hatti looks hesitant, now. Marcie feels panic over take her again, as she worries that something is going to happen.

"Your mom had you in very unstable conditions and—"

"She *needs* me!"

"Marcie, your mom neglected to feed you for what seemed like two weeks."

"I was supposed to work for my food!"

"What kind of parent makes their kid work for their food?"

It was like she was struck without being touched. She wanted to say all kinds of parents. She wanted to say that it was parents who wanted to teach their children about the truth of hard knocks, and wanted them to be independent. Those parents were the sort who had taught their children how to survive. Yet her mind raced when her thoughts returned to loving families in her situation. She thought of the parents who were trying to find jobs in hopes of actually caring for their families. She recalled how They kept their children.

"Why did you take me away from my mom?"

The woman in front of her sighed. Her eyes searched for an answer as she moved to sit next to Marcie, leaning back to figure out how to answer her question.

"When I was younger, I married a boy who I and everybody down the street thought to be the sun. They praised him every single day. Women worshipped the ground he walked on and then me for walking with him. But one day, he showed his true colors to me."

Marcie could see Hatti struggling with words as she clenched and curled her fingers together. "He struck me in ways that he felt allowed to, in certain situations, he intimidated me, manipulated me until I began to question my own judgement, and for a really long time, I believed the things he would say. I believed that the things he did were my fault."

"What happened?"

"I left him."

"Why?"

"Because sometimes, the people who say that the need us, only say that they need us to keep us for their own benefit."

Marcie looked down, and she had been unsure as to how she should react. Everything seemed to be happening fast and she couldn't find the breaks. It was like she was riding a bike down the hill and she couldn't slow down or slow herself to a stop and she was scared. She wanted her mom, but at the same time hoped that her mother would never find her or hurt her. And she barely knew the woman sitting beside her, but she had been much nicer to her than the one she had chased off. She wondered how the woman named Hatti knew that she was hungry, or potentially in danger.

Hathor, in all honesty, had almost about as much experience with children as anyone in this day and age, yet she was going to stand firm in her decision to help the little girl beside her. Everything she saw in her mothers' eyes, resembled what she saw in her ex-husbands eyes the day he knew that he was about to lose control. She recalled how he lifted a sword and gave her two options, thinking that she would choose either and grit her teeth at how juvenile he came off for throwing a tantrum. Yet like Marcie's mother, his intent had been to kill or in the very least, cause lifelong damage. She was pulled from her thoughts as a soft tapping echoed from around the corner. Balloons could be seen beyond the cubicles as they moved through a maze of what seemed to be a corporate jungle. A head of long red hair peaked over the edges and the tapping proceeded to grow louder and louder until a pale, but handsome man with his hair twisted into a braid appeared before them, throwing confetti in the air as he beamed down at the two with excitement.

"Could you make any more of a dramatic entrance?" she chided in jest.

"I could have ridden a circus ball over, but that might have taken away from the work load."

Hathor turns her attention back to Marcie with a bewildered look, sighing as she points to Loki with her thumb.

"Do you see what I have to deal with?"

As the year went by, the trio found somewhat of a disorganized balance beneath the roof that they had shared. Hathor, or Hatti, as Marcie had referred to her, would walk Marcie to school and then disappear for the rest of the day, not returning until the clock struck ten. Loki often stuck around for after school programs that had helped Marcie catch up to her peers and stuck with her as though he were a devoted father, reassuring her that everything happens at its own pace and assisting her with her basic needs. Yet she couldn't help but wonder why there seemed to be a need for separation. Marcie began to worry that Hatti no longer had time for her, let alone wanted anything to do with her.

"Why isn't Hatti home?" she asked one night.

Loki paused, looking up from a piece of math homework he had been looking over. She is unsure of what to make of his puzzled expression as he looks to her.

"That's a bit difficult to explain," he says softly, looking for the right words.

"But I suppose it would be easier to show you."

She had made her rounds accordingly, working tirelessly to

ensure that she could inspire as much compassion amongst the masses as possible. Yet lately she had begun to grow weary. There was a part of her that demanded a cease and desist, a small fraction that constantly told her to go home. Marcie was probably sitting up on the couch, hoping for her to come in and talk about her day and share stories on what silly things either had encountered. And yet, every time she returned, the little girl she had met would be passed out in her bed. But tonight…tonight seemed a little different despite being the middle of winter. The night was biting as the stars speckled the night sky, and for once in her long and seemingly endless life, she had no idea of what was to come. For some reason, she had forgotten her purpose in living on the streets to begin with.

"By the gods, Hatti, you look terrible."

Hathor looked up to find two individuals standing just several feet away from her. One, a very tall and pale handsome man, with his long red hair twisted into a braid, and the other, a little human girl who could almost be his with the twinkle in her emerald green eyes.

"For a moment I thought you were my brother," she said as Loki and Marcie approached, handing her a cup of hot cocoa.

"Old friend," Loki began. "I believe you and I have both established that to err is human."

The taller of the two smiled, moving to take her hand in his as he pressed his lips to her head. They both pulled Marcie close as if to remind her that she is safe and Hathor has a warm home to go to.

Loki looked upon his new family with a knowing smile, having nothing but hope for the coming future.

REGENT

Chapter 1

Strong arms coil firmly around her, pulling her tight against a broad chest as a well-defined chin rests on top of her head. She could feel his muscles tensing and retracting as he turns his back to the window, protecting her from the harsh rays of sunlight as they pool into the room. And all she could do is drink him in. She pulls the covers over her partner and herself as he proceeds to coil around her more, and her fingers brush along his skin in comfort.

"You're such a big baby sometimes," she chides playfully.

He says nothing.

Yet she knows that he is awake.

She listens to his steady breathing, feeling the rise and fall of his chest and simply resigns to lay there. He is obviously not ready to let her go any time soon.

James had never been one to discuss his feelings, and she hated it. It was a condition that was taught to serve some unrealistic ideal that all men had to be or act a certain way. He would only show some semblance of vulnerability in the night, when she caressed him and slowly pried him open like the closed oyster he had been raised to be. But right now, she could sense an intense desire not to let her go.

"You never told me you were married."

Her expression drops. Her pointed ears twitch as she looks for something else to talk about. Yet with how firmly he holds her to him, she could tell that she was not going to be able to get away from the subject.

"It was a long time ago," she responds.

"I guess I'm not the only one with my secrets then."

A sharp pang of guilt pierces through her like a knife. He had been slowly opening up to her and now, chances were, he was going to close himself off again. She grits her teeth and buries her head in his chest.

"What do you want to do?" she asks.

His arms loosen slightly and she manages to pull away. His expression is thoughtful, almost calculating as he tenses. And she doesn't know what to say or do.

Ariane has never been afraid of anything in her lifetime. At the same time, she had never found herself so assured of a person she had willingly brought into her life without cause for political commitment or hopes that the other would reciprocate one day without her draining herself just to appease them. James... James was the one person who did not... would not do that to her. And yet, she did not know what she was to expect with him. He had always been the strong silent type. Yet despite it all, he had never once said anything cruel, or raised a hand to her. He never put her in any danger or set impossibly high expectations of her to fulfill. He made her feel safe...

"I don't know much about the neighbors," he finally tells her.

"You've never let me in on your old life, nor have you ever

taken the time to tell me about it."

She senses that there was a 'but' in his sentence.

"I honestly don't know whether I should be angry or concerned about the situation."

Here it comes.

"Although, whatever the case, I'm still going to stick by you as you have for me."

Ariane's eyes widen in surprise.

For the longest time, she had suspected humans to reject anything or anyone that slighted them. As if to deny the hidden realities of the world around them and...

"Do you mean it?" she asks.

"I would be lying if I said I wasn't intrigued."

The way she looks at James in that moment, practically set his heart ablaze. Her cool blue eyes questioning as she wonders why he didn't reject her. And he isn't certain as to whether he should be angry or enamored by her disarming puppy like expression. He smiles softly down at her as she moves to sit upright, tucking her knees beneath her as he rises to meet the smaller of the two.

"Why?" she finally asks,

"It's been three years, Annie, why do you think?"

"Because you continue to restock the Swiss fish in the pantry?"

The statement alone was enough to bring out a howl of laughter from her partner, causing her to stiffen as her ears press back at the sudden escalation in volume. She snickers for a moment and eventually stops as he sweeps her into his arms and leans down to claim her lips in a heartfelt kiss. She parts and gazes up at him, doing her best to engrain him into her memory.

"If keeping Swiss fish in the pantry means you coming home..." he says. "Then I'll add an extra packet and some hot cocoa to get you to return home faster.”

Ariane gives James a rueful smile, as if to tell her lover that some things just weren't that simple.

They had stayed in most of the day, enjoying each other's company as if they would be apart for a while. Time had operated differently in the land of the neighbors, and Ariane wished heavily that it wouldn't be too long before she returned. She could see her lover of three years fighting to stay awake as midnight had began to ebb nearer. Slowly the clock ticked, and the tall grandfather clock pinged nearer and nearer to the stroke of midnight, and Ariane simply curled around James, squeezing her eyes shut. By midnight, she would be back in the realm of the fae, kneeling before the Unseelie king. James's arms began to loosen from her as his head bobbed to and fro. There was a soft chitter and hoot sounding from a fire escape as Ariane's eyes snapped open. James had finally fallen asleep, and a snowy owl perched on the railing just beyond the loving couple's bedroom window.

The time to leave had arrived.

Ariane slides from the bed, tucking in James with little to no knowledge as to when or if she would see him again. His chestnut hair splays about the pillow as the moon casts its rays upon his olive and lightly freckled skin. She moves to place a gentle kiss on his temple and wills him to still be alive and well upon their next meeting. And as she leaves, she can see his green eyes looking at her as if to bid farewell.

Chapter 2

James had watched as a woman exited the forest line. There was a forlorn if not hopeless expression on her face as she seemed to keep looking over her shoulder, wishing desperately for someone to come out and stop her, tell her that whatever she was walking away from had been a mistake on them. Yet despite the amount of times she looked over her shoulder and marched through the graveyard, no one had come. He quickly took note of her clothing. It was elegant yet worn and tattered as one would find in a movie about a haunted house on a hill. Her deep red hair flowed behind her as she walked with a defeated yet dignified stride. Unbeknownst to him, that he would take her under his roof and eventually fall in love. He would fall in love with that strange little point at the tip of her ears, fall in love with the way the sun warmed her olive skin or how her ocean blue eyes flickered when the light touched them at just the right angle... All these things had not processed in his mind at the time and now he was watching as she stepped through the window pane and on to the fire escape. He grimaced as he kept his eyes on her and watched as she peered obediently up at the hooded figure before her and he could see that there was a small flash of resentment in her eyes.

He wanted to call her name and plead with her not to go. He wanted her here, with him where she would be safe and loved and happy. He could tell that she was happy and he didn't want that to stop. He leaped out of bed as she was whisked away by a cloaked figure, stumbling to the window as he wriggled through the framing and out on to the fire escape. He hated that she never told him that she was married. Of all things, the most he'd known was that she had been through an abusive relationship and for some reason was tossed to the side once the person had grown bored of her. He figured that was the end and she had been free.

Now she was going back...

And he was fucking conflicted.

"Annie!" he finally cried. His voice was desperate and strained by sleep.

He called her name again, and again, pleading for her to come back. He begged her not to go and to return to where she was safe. But as he watched her fade through the alley ways and crevices of the metropolis, he knew that there was no stopping her. Finally, he made a move to go inside and hurried to get dressed. Doing his best to move with a sense of urgency before he lost his Ariane. He quickly grabbed his keys and his wallet and began to make his way toward the door. And as soon as he opened it, it was slammed shut.

"It is unwise to follow," came a voice.

James leaped back as he heard skittering before him and felt something... or someone brush along his shins. His eyes darted around and the same mass bumped against his legs again. Not wanting to deal with what or whoever it was, he reached for the door and was suddenly spun around. His back facing the entry way as though he had just come in.

"I told you," hissed the voice. "It is unwise to follow."

The man growled in agitation as he then spun back around to reach for the door. And suddenly, as though some invisible force had been dragging him backward, the door fell beyond his reach. Though, he had never been one to let anything or anyone hold him back. Be it literally or figuratively. He lifted his foot as his other heel dragged across the hardwood floor and slammed his other heel behind him on what felt to be a toe. He quickly swung his elbow back, smashing his perpetrator in the face as he quickly made a b-line for the front door, unwilling to let anyone or anything stop him from gaining any headway.

"James Isaac Henley!"

His body froze.

"Lay down."

James immediately fell to the floor, unsure of what to make of having little to no control of his body as a pair of animal like feet with silver fur padded toward him with cat like grace. He looked up to find that another, much larger individual followed closely behind them. Large yellow eyes peered down at him with contempt as a rabbit like face twisted into a displeased scowl. A lion's tail swished and snapped back and forth behind the strange creature as a pair of pointed horns protruded from their forehead.

"Now that I have your attention and have been assured you will not follow, as hard as that might have been, perhaps now I can get you to listen."

He could feel his muscles spasm and twitch. How could this tiny creature paralyze him by merely saying his name? James questioned this over and over as the small creature gestured to the larger one. There had been so much that Ariane had told him in regards to the fae. He wondered why it was that she withheld certain tidbits of information from him, why did she not tell him that to know ones full name worked on humans? Did she not want him to worry? Did she not want to scare him? Why? He questioned these things over and over again as the larger creature hoisted him into his arms. Olive green skin glowed in the light as the human spied a pair of tusks protruding from his lower lip. The large mans hair was pulled back into a braid as his face had been surprisingly handsome for one that James was beginning to assume he was.

His attention was pulled back to the tiny white fur creature as their shrill voice followed close behind.

"Our ladyship has long since called upon us in the event of a possible summons, and like many who are loyal to her, we obeyed."

James opened his mouth to speak, and just as instantly, the creature had waved their hand.

"Silence," they commanded lowly.

"I am not finished."

James had nearly been bored to death with the long lecture he had received from the small creature. He could tell that the creature's companion had seemed fairly fed up with the the creature's anecdote as well, despite not saying anything. And given that the sun had been rising, they had all been waiting through the night. Although, none of what the creature said had been askew to what he hadn't already heard from Ariane before. He knew that she led a rebellion, knew that she killed her own father and took his throne as his blood spilled onto the floor and knew exactly how long it took to build loyalties between her and a kingdom that now her supposed *husband* rules in her stead. And as he thought about it, it only angered him more and more. He hated that she was required to answer to a summons and that she was denied the choice to depart from the man completely. Only the heavens knew what James had in store for his lover's husband.

"Do you understand anything that I am telling you?" the small creature asked.

James squinted at them. If he could move and catch them, he would likely skin them alive for keeping him immobilized for so long.

"James Isaac Henley, you may speak now."

In what felt like an instant, James felt a sudden pressure tracing up his throat, heaving out in exclamation as he found himself able to move again. He shot a venomous glance to his present captor, pondering the ways he could repay him for delaying any chance of seeing Annie again. Though instead inhaled and released a soft sigh.

"You have yet to tell me why you bound and gagged me," he says lowly. "Hell, you haven't even bothered to properly introduce yourselves."

The smaller of the two creatures in his presence looked to one and other, exchanging with one and other a silent discussion before turning their attention back to him.

"My name is Kavelah," the small creature responds as they straighten themselves. "Son of Marsh and proud servant to Queen Ariane the Blood Maiden, Ruler of the Darkwood Fae... The half orc is Brom."

"And why did you bind and gag me?"

"But I did not touch you."

"You used magic on me without my consent."

Kavela narrowed their big yellow eyes at the human as their silver fur bristled on edge. James could tell that the tiny fae creature was growing agitated with him... and for some reason, the very notion of causing a small bit of inconvenience for his lovers' servant was considerably pleasing.

"So as to keep you from being an idiot."

"On whose orders?"

A heavy hand fell upon the human's shoulder and drew James's attention from his conversational adversary. The half orc was giving him a warning look. Surprise to say, it wasn't a look that was threatening. It was the sort of look a parent would give to a child when they were crossing a boundary that would cause unfavorable consequences before telling them to stop. Why? He wondered. The half orc, despite the lore of his kind being ugly, was considerably attractive and much leaner than most would consider someone born full orc would be. Though James buried the question as to why in the back of his mind, hardly feeling the need to bother with the topic.

"Brom, right?"

Brom smiled down at him, nodding softly as he patted his shoulder. He seemed gentle, despite the heavy hand. The smaller man began to study his features as soon as he turned away. Two black braids had trailed down the right side of his head while one trailed down his left. His long hair had been tied back into a wild ponytail. His skin was slightly tinted green as his eyes remained a pale grey. Were one to dress him in a hoody, one would think that he was some run of the mill king of the jocks type. Not that physical prowess was a bad thing. He was sure that the orc was seen as a great warrior among his people.

"I wouldn't expect any conversation from him," Kavelah chided, pulling James from his thoughts. "He hasn't spoken since my queen's father. "

Brom rolled his eyes and snorted in the smaller creatures general direction.

"Oh don't give me that," Kavelah quipped.

"I know perfectly well that you're quite capable of holding your own in social groups."

"So what are you, exactly?" James finally managed to ask.

The smaller of the two sighed and rolled their shoulders, as if about to give an answer to a stupid question.

"Ever hear of a phooka?"

Shapeshifters, yes. James had heard of such things, though Kavelah hardly resembled what he had imagined. They often took shapes matching the characteristics of others, right down to the voice. And the only giveaways to finding phooka were to look for a part that seemed out of the ordinary and could not be hidden. He never knew what one looked like without the disguise without properly guessing on their unique or somewhat animal like features.

"I've seen many who were glamoured," he finally responded.

"Then you know what to look for to find us, then?"

"Ariane has taught me quite a bit."

The phooka raised his brow as they gave James a very thoughtful look. And the human could practically hear the smaller being mutter as he left the room.

"Not so stupid, afterall."

Chapter 3

Crystals, books and bottles lined the dusty shelves of Ariane's old room. Specimens collected over time sat upon tables as memento mori, as if to allow the observer to imagine how the small creatures might have lived. Furs and pelts lined the edge of the bed and draped over the backs of a chaise lounge as Ariane the Blood Maiden, Queen of the Darkwood fae, leaned back with one of her old books in hand as the daylight spilled into the room like a waterfall. Since she had arrived, she had locked herself in the only provision she found security. It was the only area she had been allowed her privacy, and not even her husband could enter without her regard. She had been glad to find it left alone. She hadn't any servants to tend to the room, and such was a small if not more desirable price to pay in terms of what she planned to do once granted an audience with her husband.

An audience with her husband.....

She cringed at knowing that regrettable if not foolish decisions had been made in marrying that man. She never had to request an audience with James. She never had to wait in line or compete for his attention. He never demanded her attention when she deigned to give it and quite often allowed her some space without condition. Her mind had begun to occupy its self with hopes that he didn't follow. She prayed to her gods desperately, hoping that Kavelah had stopped him without having to hurt him and prayed dearly that she would be able to see him again.

A smile soon stretched across her features as she imagined the rest of her life with him. Sharing her life force with his and ensuring that they could both be happy. She desired for him to rule at her side, or at least appoint a new regent who she knew would rule the Darkwood Fae well.

"Lady Ariane?" she heard someone call beyond her door.

Her face twisted in contempt as she stood and glided across the room. She would not give the permission to enter unless she knew who it was that was addressing her. She swung the door open with an annoyed expression, so to let her inconvenience be known. But as she was about to open her mouth to speak, her face immediately softened. A tall, broad shouldered knight peered down at her with surprise before he leaned forward and kneeled, bowing before her with ease.

"Laurent Lauran?"

The knight gazed up with a cheeky grin. His gold eyes peered up at Ariane through strands of strawberry blond hair.

"If my lady deigns to call me Chip, anymore."

Ariane practically leapt to hug the taller fae with a soft cry of excitement, and Chip instantly stood and spun her into a hug. For the first time since she had arrived, her eyes grew misty as tears of joy ran down her face. Chip had been her only ally in her husbands' palace and often guarded her to the best of his ability. And she wouldn't deny a point in time where she might have wanted to run away with him, however his loyalty remained to the Unseelie king, and running away with him would be an act of treason.

"Oh wonderful!" announced another man's voice. "My prodigal wife finally leaves her room, and my prized captain of the guard may finally return to his post."

A man with long blond hair slowly entered the room with his

arms tucked behind his back. His heels clicked against the marble tiles as his robes flowed behind him. He peered down his nose at chip, as if to take him apart and see his worth in comparison and sneered before turning to Ariane and giving her a soft smile of acknowledgement.

"Ariane, my love," he said calmly.

"Gerard Auguste."

The Unseelie King's smile faded at Ariane's distant if not frigid tone. He reached an arm around her as his free hand tipped her chin so that she was looking up at him. His brown eyes narrowed at the defiant gaze she gave him.

"I acknowledged you," she said expectantly. "Isn't that enough?"

"I expect you to show reverence for your husband, since he has been so kind as to grant you an audience."

"An audience to say that I wish to have a divorce?"

The sounds that filled the room in that instant were enough to set everyone on edge, and neither Chip nor Ariane could see it coming. Gerard stepped away for a moment, looking away from her as he calculated his next move before he swiftly drew his palm across her face, sending her flying to the floor and crashing into the silver tea set placed beside the door to her room.

"You brought that upon yourself," he said coolly. "I figured you knew better than to slight me, darling.

Ariane slowly began to stand, processing what had been done and gave a low sigh. "So you result to taking a swing at me?" she quips.

"If it will put you in line."

"Then by all means, do the same honor for yourself, majesty."

The Unseelie Kings' eyes widened as his face twisted with rage and Ariane could only smile at her small victory. That smile soon faded as she saw him raise his hand again. Only, his next strike didn't land. His arm twisted behind his back and he was pinned to the floor. His wife's knee pressed down on his spine as he felt his arm threatened to break from her shoulder sockets. Ariane clicked her tongue as she kept the taller of the two royals pinned beneath her. Never again would she allow this man to touch her. Never again will she suffer the pain of his betrayal or the feeling of being unsure of herself or the decisions she makes for the sake of his approval. This man, ceased being her husband when he chased her from her home. And now that he had stricken her, any love or affection she might have had left for him had disappeared. He was little more than an insignificant worm who had grown too big for his britches.

The thought of killing him had finally crossed her mind. She could kill him right now for all the heartache and grievance he caused her. She could kill him for subjecting her to indescribable misery and degradation as a punishment for ever loving him.

At this point, anger and hatred had all that was left for him. She had accepted that he would never love her a long time ago, understanding... no. Hoping that if she were to return to her once vibrant home, it would be without his presence.

The blood maiden could feel as a prickly sensation erupted from her fingers as the air grew frigid. Ice begins to crystallize at the windows and spiral along the walls and cluster in the corners as they slowly congregate to her and the fae king. She can feel the ice forming at her fingertips as his hands slowly get colder and colder. To him, it must have felt like a million microscopic needles piercing into his flesh as frost slowly formed on the surface of his skin.

In that moment, she had a thought. She wondered how well the fae king would be able to manage being left alone in the woods, naked, during the dead of winter. Would he be able to survive the bite of the snow? How long would it take for him to starve? Or would he be eaten by much larger, hungrier predators before being allowed to suffer from his own famine? She couldn't retrain the sadistic smile that played across her lips at how loud his screams would be.

She leans forward, moving low enough so that her lips were inches away from his ear. Her voice dripped with venom as the room grew more and more frigid. "You are never to touch me again."

A soft hand touched the queen's shoulder, and Chip's voice drew her from her thoughts. "My queen," he says softly. "Please consider the consequences of your next actions."

She looks up at the Knight with a furious expression, which he responds with a pleading look. She knows what he is intending as her eyes search his.

He is not worth the witnesses, he means to say.

"Fine," she says in defeat.

It doesn't take too long before the ice melts and the room to warm up again as Ariane releases Gerard. She flocks to Chip with ease as she apologizes to him in silence. Chips eyes fall on his king, who is now regarding him with thoughtful resolve.

"Lock her in her room," he orders. "She is to dine alone, tonight."

The Unseelie King soon left the room, leaving a sense of apprehension for the two. The energy in the air had lost it's positivity in the skirmish. There was nothing in that moment that the two could find to recover from it, and Ariane sighed.

"I guess you've gone from queen to prisoner, then," he says lowly. And Chip can only pat her back reassuringly.

"Bright side is, you have me, right?"

Ariane smiles at him, envious of his ability to find the silver lining of the situation. "I guess it's not too bad."

The hours had passed as her friend kept her company, only leaving her room once or twice to make his rounds. Each time, he enters without any need to knock. Yet as day fell to night, something ominous had been reaching through the back of Ariane's mind. Chips returns continued to get further and further spaced out.

Why? Questions of what might have been occurring spun through her mind. Was Chip dead? Had he done something that was considered treason? Was Gerard assigning him to near impossible tasks? All of these questions raced through her mind as she circled back and forth to every single one.

She leaped as she heard a loud knock at her door.

Odd. Chip didn't need to knock.

She looked through her peep hole, spying the area with curiosity as she looked for who might have been knocking and found no one. She heard something brush at the floor and tap against her foot. A tray of food had been placed atop two hat boxes, along with an envelope with contents addressed to her. She set her tray to the side and began to open the first box. A top hat had been neatly placed inside the box's contents, a musty yet coppery smell filled her senses and soon she was filled with a sense of dread. She quickly opened the second box and the earth-shattering scream that she released echoed through the room. The blood stained strawberry blond hair that peaked out from the box was enough indication as to why Chip hadn't returned. Ariane's screams faded in to cries and evolved into mournful wail's as she fell to her knees and doubled over from the shock. It was as though the ground had been pulled from beneath her and all that was left was her rapid decline.

The seconds ticked by and all the fallen queen could now do was lay on the cool ground, curled around the hat box containing her newly departed friend's head, and hoping that this was some twisted little prank of his.

Alas, she had been wrong.

And this was all that she had left of him.

Hours had seemed to have gone by. All Ariane could remember of those hours were that she had eventually faded into a dreamless sleep after losing what hope she had of having an ally in the palace. A great wave of emotions washed over her at that point. Rage and sorrow had seemed to be the more pronounced of them and her nails angrily scraped against the floor as she then stood and began to storm through the room, shouting and screaming profanities that she knew would reach down the hall and out her window. She threw bottles and books at the walls and destroyed the large mirror that had stood in her room long before she had inhabited it. This caused her pause as the glass shattered in to a thousand pieces, revealing a passage she had not noticed before.

She turned her attention to the broken glass and contemplated her next steps as she craned her neck to peer down the new dark corridor she was now intent to explore.

Yet as she looked around her room she took notice of the bottles and wondered around, thinking that the mirror would just continue to be a broken mirror with every instant she had turned around. Instead what seemed to have been broken mirror pieces were shards of glass were thick and so deep red they appeared black until light pooled in their curves and revealed their secrets. Sigils had danced upon the broken glass and Ariane had been left speechless as she turned to face the scene before her, lifting the envelope and opening it to reveal the message inside.

> *To remind you of your place and the*
> *consequences of your actions. Do you wish for*
> *another to die, because of you?*
> *—G.Auguste, Your Husband*
> *and rightful king of the Unseelie Court*

Ariane had already been consumed with rage at this point. Instead, in that moment, she had made an oath to herself. Promising that she would leave, even if it killed her, and neither Chip, nor the top hats' original owner, will have died in vain.

She eyed the newfound corridor and narrowed her eyes, taking one step forward, followed by another and another before she found herself descending into the passage of what appeared to be an endless void. Of all the things the situation had come to, Ariane found little hope in staying or getting Gerard to agree to her terms.

She recalled a situation like this when she was younger. Her father's old palace had been riddled with secret passages and doorways that led to deep corridors that seemed to lead to nowhere. Those passages often helped make her life at least a bit more bearable. For as long as she stayed in her room, no one would find out about her private escape. And as she got older, she found that having such a passage would turn her prison into her sanctuary.

The twists and turns seemed almost endless as Ariane could only navigate through the darkness if she had a wall to cling to. She hardly minded the spiderwebs or the feeling of tiny creatures skittering along her skin, and the deeper she went, the more common they had become. Ariane persisted forward, refusing to turn back.

The Cat

ndlessly I question what my exodus may prove and endlessly I ponder my purpose as though my life depended on it. At night I lay awake and stare at the ceiling, watching as shadows dance along the walls and potentially creep out of my bedroom window for a late-night stroll. The streets are only barely lit where it matters, though the alleys and vacant lots where nature and overbrush had lain claim seem to hold the most promise. This in and of itself helps with my insecurities, brings me comfort. It allows me to think clearly and plan ahead for what other steps to take, as apprehensive as I may be as to whether or not such motions may work. I dread the possibilities of such plans potentially leading to starvation.

These are the thoughts that race through my mind as fingers

brush through my hair and whisper sweet nothings to me. I adore the comfort. I adore the compliments and the endless gifts of admiration and deeply take advantage of the liberties I am given. Some would call me spoiled for openly speaking of such notions, however, the sunlight upon my skin distracts me from those unpleasantries. It will hardly matter in the next five seconds. Theo, the new boy next door seems to have said such things, despite taking a liking to me. He is very presumptuous in his approaches and constantly assumes that, based on my interests, I am willing to lay down for him. Also, my caretaker finds this more humorous than the crazed woman who stomps loudly down the way.

No matter.

It is a glorious morning now that I have relieved myself of my pessimism and my food dish is finally full.

I'm certain I had nearly starved.

HOPELESS

I have everything I could possibly want. I keep telling myself so, even though it means telling myself a complete and utter lie. And as I sit and stare upon the crumbling walls of a nearly condemned house with no proper sewage or running water. There is no money to fix things. There is nothing that is pertinent to survival. Banging my head against the wall, seems the only viable thing to maintain my sanity as the anxiety and poor state of mind seem to grow in a way that I don't want it to. The nightmares are more frequent. The fear that I may lose everything screams louder and no amount of music or distraction can possibly drown it out.

I am damned.

I am damned if I stay. I am damned if I leave.

And I fear that getting out may be more difficult this time.

I remember when I was very small. Both my father and grandmother's houses were like museums. Yet one breathed with more life than the other. My grandmother's house was very much alive, with lush gardens filled with hibiscus and honeysuckle. She had a lemon tree that grew in the far corner and small patches of jasmine growing wild as chickens would come in and out. And on some days the sun would shine through the windows and illuminate the halls and the living room as though my grandmother's home were some grand cathedral, or a sanctuary filled with promises of immeasurable joy and laughter.

I wish I could say the same for my father's home.

While beautiful to some on the surface, everything held a much darker meaning in my eyes. There was no promise of joy or laughter. Just beautiful things in glass cases for the world to see. Perhaps, on some occasions I would find an old painting mounted on the wall. Other times I would see frightening masks and artifacts that had been stolen from their homeland. The only real semblance of color that I remember of his house was a Turkish dagger that he had found during a tour in the middle east. He never told me where he had found it. Only that the man who had sold it to him said that it had belonged to a group of nomads who had lost to him in a gambling match. The sheath was the color of vintage paper, patinaed by time into a shade neither grey nor white. But suspended somewhere in between. The hilt glinted sterling silver and could easily catch the eye of guests when they saw it. Unfortunately, such a thing was not enough for me to find a sense of joy, nor laughter in my fathers' home. It served more of a reminder as to what my expectations were. How to act, how to not embarrass the head of the household and how to stay silent, yet still manage to be interesting. It made me feel like a bird in a cage. And when my grandmother died, that's all I felt I was. And as time progressed and the houses changed, they always somehow stayed the same. Eventually they began to reflect how I began to see myself.

Now, as an adult, I find myself in a predicament. I know that there is conflict and challenges, but my will to overcome both is almost non-existent. The years of expectations have run me ragged and I have no accomplishments to show for it. I am weary of others. My ability to trust is faulty and I would be lucky if I could find some semblance of joy for only a moment. But now is not the time. As I hear screaming from up and down the hall of this crumbling house, I feel helpless. There are no words to comfort me as of this moment and I am not sure if any ever will.

It's difficult, focusing on the good things in your life when there has already been so much bad.

I could have everything I possibly want. I try to keep telling myself so, even though I have nothing. I come from nothing and I have no legacy. And as I sit and stare upon these walls of a crumbling house, with no sewage or running water, I wallow in my own potential grave. I have no way to get out. I don't have the money or connections I need to get out.

I am damned.

I am damned if I stay.

I am damned if I leave.

And I am unsure if escape is viable at this point.

The Uphill Battle

It's funny when others say that standing, walking, and breathing is easy. They've obviously never had to claw their way through the mud while trying to make it to the top of the hill. And during the climb, have their hands bitten by poisonous insects that plague one's thoughts and bring them to a mental state of unrest or have heavy boots stepping all over them both intentional and not. And the heavier the footfall, the more inclined its owner is to hurt, to cause harm, to stop the climber from reaching what it is that they want to achieve. No one will know what the motivation is that will cause that amount of pain. Few will forgive it and will let it roll off their back.

For me, personally, it is a matter of timing. It is a matter of whether dwelling will solve anything or bring importance to an issue or a topic. And I like to think of ways to approach things that have happened in the past, so I can use it in the future. But I still acknowledge that no matter what I do, I am still on that uphill slope. My face is still buried in the mud and I am no better than anyone else. I can't deny that I've hurt others unintentionally. I cannot say how deep the trenches go with others, because I am not them. What I can say, however, is that no one realizes how easy it is to fall until they must start climbing their way back up on their own. And frankly, I envy those who have yet to do so. I envy those who have others to lift them out of the mud and pull them back to the top of the hill, but I also find them to be irritating. Because those people are the people who have taken too many things for granted in my eyes.

You can tell who they are.

They're all over the place and in their mind, everything is easy.

The most belligerent are the people who say "Your disability is in your head. Stop being so lazy." Or "Medication is a gateway to codependence, you don't need medication to keep your seizures in check." These people have had many advantages in life that, to me, deprives them of compassion. They have never lost the ability to walk or to do the things that they want without worrying about how it affects them. They've never had to figure out ways to manage their stress in a way that wouldn't cause a cumulative shutdown. And that's only the medical part of it all.

You don't, you can't, and you are, are all double-edged swords that can bring both the giver and receiver to their knees and push their faces back into the mud if used improperly. The giver can destroy their reputation and harm the receiver. But the giver can be one of the few who can help convince the receiver of the positives.

You don't have to give a toxic person your time.

You can go home and take care of that novel or painting that you've been working so hard on.

You are a talented and good-hearted human being who deserves so much in this life.

These things being said can do a lot of good for a person who has been clawing their way through the mud all week. These things can do a lot of good.

I remember life with my grandmother and how she would constantly encourage me to continue drawing or reading something out loud. I remember how she would describe my feet as being firmly planted on the ground and how she would come along with a hairdryer and an umbrella if it dared to turn into mud. And one day when I asked her what would happen if it became too much, she looked me in the eye and said, "Well, if it becomes too much, I will hand you the blow dryer and the umbrella." Upon hearing this, I began to feel a part of myself sink. My five-year-old brain began to feel as though I had to be perfect for her to love me.

"But…" she would begin again. "I will still be here with an extra umbrella and hairdryer, if you begin to get tired."

I don't know if she realized at the time. But those words always seemed to make my day when they came from her.

It wasn't until I was seven when the rain started to pour harder in my life. And by age eight I was already struggling to stay on top of the hill and by twenty-six, I'm still struggling to make the halfway point. I guess it comes from feeling as though I had been forgotten in one corner, cloaked in cobwebs and decades of dust, having been treated as a survivor merely by default, by being over-looked, silent and unobtrusive, not big enough to be an imposition and so allowed to remain—a receptacle of memories, an eye witness to everything that came before... as dramatic as it sounds.

The thing that many don't seem to realize is how easy it is to fall. It's one thing when someone is constantly there to lift you up or be able to manage your own solid grounding. It's another to lose it all and struggle to keep yourself up. It's another not to have anyone there or someone there who lacks empathy or compassion. Especially if those people are your own parents or family members. And you become closed off. Which makes the mud deeper and more difficult to manage, and it gets to a point where you just want it all to go away. And when you try to push and power through it, the trying stops being enough and it eventually fades into disappointment. You start to doubt yourself and whatever expectations you may have had of beating that damn hill are never met.

And it gets to a point where you want to take your own life.

Looking in the mirror, I recollect the times I have. I wouldn't wish anything that goes on in my brain onto anybody. I see the struggles that many have on a daily basis and my heart goes out for them. And I almost want to ask what they went through. Sure, depression and many cases of mental illness are genetic; however, in many other instances, there are triggers. There are root causes and those who are neurotypical are none the wiser.

For those of you, who like me, are struggling with that same damn hill. I see you.

I see your pain.

I see your struggle.

And I am proud that you have managed for this long.

People have died on this hill and have been buried by the mud. Many are beneath our fingers or have been delivered by what flowers grow near the top.

That could be you.

That could be me.

But it isn't.

We are here.

And we are fighting to stay alive.

WHAT HAPPENS NEXT

I used to wonder how far this nation will go if we allow the folks in power to keep a morally corrupt president in office. In Donald J. Trump's four year term, I have seen countless offences committed under the guise of false patriotism. Internment camps have been filled beyond capacity, beyond what is considered humane without clean drinking water or toiletries, while its residents are treated like nothing more than senseless beasts. And this is only scratching the surface. President Donald J. Trump idolizes Hitler in ways that I can't even imagine. He presses his ideals on others, forces protestors out in the cold and even makes fun of Autistic reporters. And that was during his first year of presidency. I constantly see people commenting on things that speak out against him and offences that he has made toward women and non-white folk. More often than not, the most common is "Fake News". His biggest atrocity, however, is interning immigrants and having ICE go to the homes of immigrants who sought nothing more than asylum from their countries of origin. But he's not going for the white European immigrants. He's going for the Latinx, the Syrian, the Iranian and more. He is doing what Bush senior had put into motion and Bush Junior had acted upon. He is using fear tactics and propaganda to spread lies and hate about a specific group of people and he knows what effect it will have. He knows how his supporters will react and how they as his followers will make an attempt to militarize and oppress these people to no avail.

During my time in Virginia, I have obtained employment at Colonial Williamsburg, added a new partner to my family, and said new partner had obtained employment at the Jamestown settlement. And what we have noticed at both of those locations is this: The interpreters and the beliefs that both places have portrayed are entirely different compared to one and other. Colonial Williamsburg not only serves as a living history museum like Jamestown, but it is also the campus location of the college of William and Mary. Many of William and Mary's alumni like wearing MAGA caps and pressing their political beliefs onto others. I remember sitting in Panera with Kayti, my new partner and over hearing a couple of young women talking about the point of civil rights. They continuously questioned "What's the point of it?" and would make passing comments like "Maybe the Civil Rights Act should be abolished. We don't need it." I wanted to rise up. I wanted to say something, but my main concern was with Kayti. My main concern was about how she would feel if I made a public spectacle of myself. She was already having a bad day as was. She didn't want for it to get any worse. So I asked if she would like to leave, and we left. And to this day I still see many people like those women. Donning their MAGA caps and looking down their nose at others they deem lesser. And I continue to wonder, just how many more people will be targeted. How much more will America unravel as a country and how many more people will die just to obtain the ideals of the few. It's not the America that I was promised growing up. It's not the America that the American citizens need. And the back bone of this country was made up of immigrants. Many from China, Italy, Spain, Ireland, Scotland, Russia, France and so on. Its backbone thrives on the people trying to make a life for themselves... or at least it used to. Now, we have to worship those who were born with a silver spoon in their mouth. Those who have never had to work a day in their lives. And it angers me. It angers me that a bunch of white guys in office have so much while everyone else has so little. And it angers me that many of the white Americans that come in to Yorktown or Jamestown find the information they obtain completely and utterly pointless. And it's because of them that we have the bastard in office. It's because of them that "Immigrant Detention Centers" are packed beyond capacity with little food or water or even basic hygiene components. And I fear what they will do to those people and I begin to think of a book that I had read once. And many of them are likely thinking the same thing that many of the characters in said book had thought. "Why me?"

There have been many occasions where I have seen history repeat its self. And there are many who believe that history is just history and that it means nothing. The united states of America is hardly as united as it used to be. Its beginnings were good. The separation of church and state was good. Because it meant that one could be allowed to press their religious beliefs upon another person for the sake of a political agenda. Yet, here we are. Abortion is being made illegal, women are being arrested for miscarriages and losing babies to gunshot wounds. These women have done absolutely nothing wrong. These people trying to cross the border and seeking asylum, have done nothing wrong. It is not illegal to seek asylum. It should not be illegal to have a miscarriage. But it should be illegal to wrongfully incarcerate an entire group of people. It should be illegal to neglect the people you lead because they are not wealthy. And it *should* be illegal to deny benefits to families and folks in need for the sake of lining your own or some other billionaire's pockets.

And so I wonder....

How many more will be arrested? How many more people will be put in to an internment camp if nothing is done right away? How many more people will wonder if they will live to see tomorrow?

And as I look at the world as it is today, I wonder. I remember the meaning of the word tyranny. I know what an internment camp looks like. I know what genocide and war looks like.

America as we know it is at the seventh stage of genocide, and there is only a few more stages to go before the government tries to cover it up and deny that it even happened.

I exhaust myself in trying to make sense of it all. I hate that what is happening now is similar to Nazi Germany and the burning of roam. Although I don't feel that the current POTUS knows how to play any instruments seeing as the only talent that he actually has is running his mouth, and he can't even do that well. I especially exhaust myself over how many will hear about this time period. Will it be seen as just *another bad presidency*? Or will children and adults stop and actually learn from it?

These are the sort of things that go through the head of someone whose citizenship can be taken away in any point in time. And having been born on Guam, that time may be soon. And then maybe I will end up in a concentration camp, myself.

With where this country is headed, guarantees are but a fools game. You live, you breath, you watch and you learn.

LAMENTING

There are no words that I can use to even remotely describe the grief that I am going through as of the moment.

She's gone, I try to tell myself.

But then I ask myself, "Where?"

After going through every turn and motion in my head, after trying to make sense of it all, I still can't find the motivation or good sense to even believe that someone I had put so much faith and trust into had simply vanished.

It's a rare thing for me to do. My friends and trusted colleagues are few and far between and I generally prefer to keep it that way. And I question as to whether or not it is fair. I question whether or not I should let others in after the amount of things I have gone through. I have put my faith into people who have taken very serious matters and turned them around to use as tools against me. I have been abused and lied to by people I was supposed to trust and have even made a firm decision not to trust others until they have shown me that I could actually confide in them. And when I do, it comes with the trust that I give to those who I know and feel will not treat me as others have. Who will not turn their back on me and who will treat me as though I am valid and I will give them the exact same respect.

I will not deny that a recent event has left me stunned and down for the count. I will not deny that the writing intended *just* for this moment was completely put to the side because I could not continue with it.

Why should I?

After all of the pain and the hurt and the misplaced trust, why should I continue with something when I know that trying to distract myself from the issue that affects me is only going to make the pain worse. It's only going to produce bad writing, soulless prompts that have little to no place in my mind right now.

My dear reader….

There will be times where you will find parts of your life that are full of splendor. You will meet people who will hurt you, people who will love and leave you, but then find those who will share similar pains and say "So how do we learn and move forward from this pain?" The people who do that are the most wonderful people. And sometimes, them leaving will be too soon because you—having found a person who understands your struggle apart from their own, but not fault you for it—is often one of the greatest friends you will ever have. Sometimes, life happens. Sometimes there are unforeseen circumstances that tear that friend away... be it suicide, an abusive and controlling parent, etc... Circumstances like those are often beyond your control. And as much as you want to fight it, as much as you want to take that persons hand and pull them toward you, where you will know that they will be safe, it sometimes just doesn't work that way.

Sometimes, you end up sitting at a computer through blurred vision because you know that you are trying so hard not to let the situation get to you. Because it is so fresh in your mind that you can't do anything to fight it off. You begin to hate yourself for not doing more and even blame yourself.

Originally, this prompt was going to be about a little boy who grows up with his family in a small cottage in the woods. Who everyday sees a swarm of dragonflies dancing out in the field until the sun sets beyond the horizon, until one day he decides to join them. One of the dragonflies takes notice and eventually reveals that the dragonfly isn't a dragonfly at all… but rather a pixie. The pixie invites the little boy to dance with her when ever he likes and even begins to sit upon his front porch for a conversation. And as the little boy grows into a man, the two begin to fall for one and other, until one day signs of a harsh winter begin to reveal themselves, the grass is painted white with a thick frost and the days begin to grow colder and colder. The young man tries to convince the pixie to stay with him and stay out of the cold, but the pixie in earnest, refuses.

Months go by and the pixie doesn't show, the young man calls out to the name she had given him and people tell him that she doesn't exist. Some have even begun to think that he had possibly gone mad. And eventually, the young man began to believe that that was the case. He had been so secluded through out his life, growing up alone with no friends or company to call his own, so that had to be it. Until one day, as the snow began to melt, something had caught his eye. A doll who looked exactly like the pixie had lain still at the far corner of the field he used to play in as a boy. The skin had grown tarnished with dirt and the eyes a dull grey… to which the young man thinks for a moment. Perhaps it wasn't so much that the pixie was dead but rather that she had never been alive. And her disappearance those months earlier had been the death of what might have been a solitude based delusion? A case of cabin fever? For even he knew that it is impossible to love one who isn't there or never existed to begin with.

My conclusion of the story was going to be of the young man, now much older and wiser—having never been married—walking along the forest with a dog at his side, passing by the same field and watching the dragon flies dance until the evening, and then deciding, "She was real to me."

I will admit....

I had written three versions of that story, and when I had finally finished the final draft, I had counted well over 3500 words. 3500 words to describe the life and death of an impossible yet bittersweet romance that described loss. I had listened to Madame Butterfly and Anna Karenina in the background to set the right mood, taking the sexuality of the two away from them. Because not every romance revolves around sexuality or erotic tone. Some romances evolve from long standing respect and mutual friendships. Some romances revolve around friendships and to have a platonic romance is just as powerful as one that is sexual. And as I write this, I think about the last thing I said to my friend. I never even told her how much I loved her or how much she meant to me.

I never knew how much not having her in my life would hurt until she was actually gone.

And even now, as this is being published or read, I hate myself for taking her presence for granted. And it's amazing how much it hurts when someone near and dear to you is gone in a heartbeat. So, reader, if you have someone who you deeply cherish—be it romantically or platonically—please know that every moment with them is a gift. Every time you speak, the words you say could be your last. And know that there is a friend who sees you the same way as well, and loves you just the same and wants to hold on to you for dear life, no matter what.

I, a writer whom you've likely never met, give my love to you.

I cherish you.

And anyone who says otherwise may read this and find proof

that there is someone in the world who loves and cherishes your existence. It's the proof that I needed. It's the proof that Micha needed.

And I will be heartbroken when your star goes out.

To Love and to Cherish

The night was as bleak as any other stormy night. The clouds overhead would drown out the stars as rain bucketed down upon Venice. Thunder clapped in the distance as the streets were occasionally illuminated by bright flashes of lightning.

It had been nights like these that Helios DiStrega loved the most, however. They were the sort of nights where they could at least pretend to be human, despite being otherwise. On nights like these, they would have the fire roaring as they sat upon a faded Turkish rug. The walls had been aligned with bookshelves, filled to the brim with rare content that many would not have access to in this day and age. Yet one could see the occasional gap here and there, spaces that Helios had climbed to in order to reach the book they had been itching to read next. Especially with the ongoing storm outside.

They would hunch over one book after the other, wrapped in a knitted wool blanket as they sat before their hearth. Should one walk into the room at that moment, they would say that they looked like a beautiful gargoyle. Their eyes gleamed in the light of the fire, as reflective rays added a striking florescence to their emerald green eyes, almost as though they were a cat intent on watching their prey as they fixed themselves upon the literary content before them. If one had allowed them, they would sit like that for hours….days, even as they refrained from blinking. Turning one page after the other and consuming tome after tome of forgotten literature.

"Have you even fed?" comes a voice.

Within moments, a man with golden skin and gleaming amethyst eyes emerged from the darkest corner of the room, casting his shadow beside the smaller being upon the floor. His wavy snowy white hair hung just over his eyes as a look of concern drew a pout from his full lips.

Mahtob had always held this kind of concern for them. And the way he currently hovered caused the younger of the two to lean back in reminiscence, recalling a time when they had been human. They had just met him without any inkling as to the predator he so attempted to convey. And they had gained the sort of reputation that one would expect of a level-headed merchant, as opposed to their prior life. But the way they had met would have been seen as unconventional, given the situation and the approach. Needless to say, Helios DiStrega, had remained married to him to this very day. Vampires had been the sort who, when they married, never had to worry about aging physically. Instead, those who missed being human, reserved an odd sense of nostalgia or envy….Helios had been one of them.

"I mixed some type O in my Darjeeling well over fifteen minutes ago." They say softly. They return their gaze to their book and continue reading. "It's gotten a bit cold for my taste, but if you wish to take some…"

A sigh of relief and a short laugh.

"No, no, I prefer lapsang, if you remember," he reminds.

"Did you?" Helios smirks. "And here I thought the build up in years had been making me senile."

"There are other things that can make you senile, little

rabbit."

A salacious grin pulls at the corners of their mouth, exposing a pair of sharp canines as their expression changes from focused to suggestive and playful. And without looking up from their book they feign disinterest as their husband drops beside them. They turn a page, pretending not to notice before feeling his breath on their ear.

"Aren't you curious as to what it is?" he enquires.

His voice is low and husky. His fingers slowly brush along theirs as he leans closer and closer, moving to take their attention away from their book. His free hand reaches up to gently caress their chin and turn their head so that his eyes are meeting theirs. And instead of irritation, all he could find in his spouses' eyes in that moment was adoration. He watches as they search his, licking their lips to see just what he intends to do next, what he plans or any movements that might give his next act away, but finds nothing as he remains still. He smirks as they fight every thought and temptation to ask, but hide his smirk as they fail miserably.

"I cannot answer unless you ask, dear one," he finally teases.

Helios pouts up at him and gives a pleading wine. Mahtob doesn't relinquish his grip as he turns them to face him, yet keeps his hold upon them. Never wavering or blinking as they wait. He knows that the delightful torment of their spouse could go on forever if Helios allows it, and he has always been known to be a very patient man. Mainly because his lack of answering and managing to keep a hold on a person somehow brought a sick sense of joy to him.

"Mahtob..." Helios breaths out, doing their best to not let their voice strain. "Please."

"Please what?" he asks, leaning down to gently nip and suck on their lower lip. He keeps a subtle grin as he hears them whimper and try to claim his lips. He draws back before they can manage to do so and gives them a playful smirk.

"That's not fair," they huff.

"All is fair in love and war, Helios."

It doesn't take long before either of them are incapacitated by the other. The hours go by with fingers entwined with one and other, sweet promises of eternity or something close are said between breaths and cries to the heavens while leading to an eventual climax to the evening and bodies intertwined. Mahtob pulls their spouses body close, nuzzling his face into a head full of raven hair as he dances his fingers along their hip. They curl up beside him, sleeping peacefully as though there weren't a care in the world and recalling how he had met them.

He had been a vampire for well over a century by that point. He had wondered all through out eastern Europe aimlessly, wishing desperately that someone—anyone, might know how to kill him. The original person he had given up his humanity for had been long gone and everything seemed pointless. Nothing mattered. Until one day, he had heard shouting in an alley way, something about someone's mother being a prostitute and turning another ones mother into a homosexual and whatnot. And while he felt that there was hardly a need to mention or blame such things on the other person, it was likely best to stop and take a step back there….or in the very least have someone intervene. He turned the corner to observe the commotion to find a young woman glaring up at another woman who had very recently given her a black eye. The young woman was an odd looking little thing who seemed to like picking fights with people larger than she was, yet in a way, lovely to look at. He could tell that she would have an advantage in the fight with the trousers she wore and the knife and flintlock at her side, but he questioned why it was that she hadn't been using either. Her black hair had been a mess and she had a black eye with a bloody nose and a busted lip. Something that many gentlemen would find almost unseemly. Yet when all was said and done, something pulled at him, pushed him to approach and gods was he thankful that he had. As he put his hand on her shoulder to ask whether or not she had been alright, he had found that what little breath he had left to give had been stolen from him as the young woman whipped around, cocking her flintlock as she pointed a knife to his throat.

"Not the smartest thing to do, sir…" she warns. "Lest you have a death wish, I suggest you don't go about sneaking up on people."

"And what if I do?" he draws out. "What if I want to die?"

Those very words spilled out of him like a waterfall. Embarrassment and shame had begun to consume him. He hadn't meant to say such things to a complete stranger, no matter how much it would have caught them off guard. No, he shouldn't have said such things to begin with. Yet there she was, caught off guard, expression softening yet still serious as she placed her blade and firearms in her holsters before straightening herself.

"Then you should probably pick a different path."

As she turned to leave, he couldn't help but stare after her in wonder. If he had chosen to die that day, he wouldn't have discovered her for who she was and married them. He wouldn't have had his son, or hold their hand as the strain of child birth nearly took their life away, they wouldn't have become a vampire and he would have lost his humanity a long time ago. It would be a great disservice to say that a single person lacked great influence to change another's mind, like saying the light of a candle lacked the ability to illuminate a room.

In a way, Helios had saved him.

Not that he would admit it.

He moved to tuck them further under the covers and kissed their forehead before wrapping his arms further around them, caressing every curve of their body as if to record every last detail of their being to memory.

He was thankful for having them in his life. Thankful for making his immortality more interesting as the years went by and thankful for their patience with him.

Eternity was a very long time.

Why not spend it with the person he loved coming home to the most?

CALL ME KITTEN

He hadn't been sure how long they had been riding. All he knew was that it would get them further away from where they began, and for what reason? He had just barged into her room late in the night and offered his hand with a choice. He didn't pause to explain the blood or dirt on his clothes. He didn't bother telling her what he did to her brother, though the bastard deserved it.

Instead, he shut down his business, cashed out what funds he'd accumulated over his long life and destroyed what evidence of his existence that had once been.

"Where are we?" Lucrezia Markova asked as she pulled her helmet off. He had slowed for a pit stop at the nearest gas station, intent on filling the tank of the black 2004 Kawasaki and speeding off as soon as they were able. He had to estimate that they were somewhere between Alexandria and Richmond, given the density of the trees. Definitely a good distance away from Seattle.

"We're at a seven-eleven," he finally responded.

"Stowe…" she grumbled back and he rolled his eyes.

"What Lu?"

Stowe had forgotten how long ago the sun had set and turned

to face his shorter companion. She had been narrowing her eyes with her arms folded over her chest. Her face twisted into a displeased scowl as her lips formed into a soft pout.

In all honesty, it was moments like these that caused Stowe to take a step back and steel his breath. He was never sure how to react to her when she was like this, without wanting to take her somewhere dark and secluded. He could feel his insides flutter as the thought of her bare and pinned beneath him emerged from the deep crevices of his mind. He reveled in the idea of her chest rising and falling as sweat trickled down her curves while she writhed beneath his ministrations. These sorts of things nearly drove him to the edge, yet were better left for a more reasonable time.

"You haven't spoken to me in over a month."

Had it been that long?

"Ah."

"Have I done something?"

"No."

"Then what?"

Lucrezia's violet eyes glowed up at him, unrelenting as they bore in to his own. What was he to say? What was he to do? He tried to turn his head to look away, yet she reached up to coax him back. He wondered how she saw him in that moment. He wondered what it was about him that kept her by his side, and why was she so trusting?

"Why do you question so little of me?"

Stowes eyes filled with a pained curiosity in that instant. And the smaller of the two hadn't been confident as to how she should answer him. Lu had little to no reason to question him as he had been nothing other than forthright to her. He never lied and never hid the truth without good reason, but other than that, they did question why they trusted so much. Could it be that he was real? Lu was never quite so superficial as to stay with someone for their good looks, such things would be a matter of ill judgement. Was it because he liked keeping her around and she liked being wanted for something other than someone elses incestuous desires or needs? She caught her reflection in the security mirror of the gas station and gave a low sigh. The person looking back at her was a waspy little thing with short black hair and skin pale enough for her to seem ill. Her brother said it came close to a mix between ivory and alabaster, and yet she saw it more as a curse. A reason to be touched by unwanted hands as he had proven to do. She began to ruminate over the last time she had been with him... the things he whispered and the way she felt. In many ways she despised herself for not leaving when she was able. But after she met Stowe....

"You make me feel safe," she finally answered. "I don't feel judged around you and you never take advantage of what vulnerability I allow myself around you."

She moved to brush a stray lock of strawberry blond hair from his face. Watching his grey eyes as they bore into her, as though he were a lover asking for reassurance that she wants him for him. She immediately pulled the breaks in her mind. Stowe was not her lover, and thinking that he was was a dangerous path to follow. And in that moment, she broke her gaze and looked down, nursing the self inflicted wound she had caused herself.

"That is to say I trust you."

Stowe wanted so desperately to sweep her up into his arms right then. He wanted to hold her close and kiss her in a way that said how much she meant to him. Yet he did his best to refrain from taking the situation for granted for his own selfish reasons or motives. He ached for her to make the first move and would remain content with what he had with his companion if she decided against it. She was a silly little thing that he had grown to endear, despite knowing how a younger version of him would never have dreamed of developing romantic interest, yet here he was. And he already had, despite himself. Needless to say, it hadn't been as though he hadn't tried to avoid the bloody endeavor. It wasn't his decision to be caught mid transformation as the sun set. It wasn't as though he were forcing Lucrezia to stay. And looking at it, he could easily have chosen any one of the models or Hollywood actresses in his reservoir and any one of them would have been at his feet as either a man *or* a woman. Yet it was this too polite little mouse with her too cute little button nose and her damn stubborn and bookish behavior, always questioning the reality of things or trying to make an iota of sense of whatever situation or person she came across. And he had been around her for so long that he hadn't been sure as to whether or not it delighted or infuriated him.

He forced himself to sneer at her, wrinkling his nose as though the vampire had placed a raw piece of durian root beneath it.

"A little misplaced, don't you think?"

"I think you give yourself less credit than you're due."

A long pause followed before Stowe attempted to retort. Nothing could be said. No wise cracks or snide rebuttles. Nothing about Lucrezia's character.

Given the situation, it was being made pertinently clear that his companion was growing more and more frustrated with him by the second. And usually, the two would break into an argument. He would try to make his points and she would turn it around with her own oppositions. Needless to say, Lu had been surprised that it hadn't gotten to that situation as of yet.

"What if I don't deserve it?"

A smile stretched across Lucrezia's lips as she for the very first time pulled the Nephilim into a tight embrace. She nuzzled her face into his chest and took in his scent, finding comfort in knowing that she was with her master. Her heart leaped with joy the moment she felt his strong arms wrap around her waist. She thanked the stars that the two had stopped for her to hunt some time back, as she had no desire to lose herself to her thirst. She didn't want to hurt him as the world had already done.

"Well, isn't this sweet?" came a voice.

It was unfamiliar to Lucrezia, despite being sweet with a venomous edge.

Stowe looked up from the embrace and pulled his companion tighter against him, doing his best to protect her, as a pair of piercing blue eyes gleamed from the dense brush of the forest across the street. And before he knew it, a woman with bronze skin and fiery red hair, clad in black leathers emerged from the darkened path. Her boot heels clicked against the pavement as the gas station lights further illuminated her features. Upon recognizing her, Stowe nearly lost his composure, releasing Lucrezia and dropping to his knees in apology. The vampire of the two looked up to study the woman, taking note of her gold tipped ears and manicured claw tipped fingernails. And from what Lucrezia could tell, there was no sign of ill intention, despite the displeased expression on the other woman's face. And as she pulled to a stop, Lu could only raise her brow at the air of disappointment that the stranger had been giving off. The woman glanced down at her and folded her arms before scowling back at Stowe.

"It would have been much sweeter if you had announced you and yours upon entering my territory, but I digress."

Stowe bowed his head respectfully, placing his right hand over his heart and refraining from looking up. From what Lu had been seeing, the woman he had been kneeling before had been his regent. And usually, he never kneeled—let alone bowed—to anyone.

"My lady Ariane, I—"

"Don't kiss ass in front of your Girlfriend, little boy," the Sheriff chided. "It's demeaning."

Stowe sputtered and Lu could feel her cheeks heat up. Lucrezia never once assumed that Stowe saw her as anything more than a supernatural ward. And even then, he treated her more as a comrade or confident than anything else. She took a breath and slowly released as the red haired woman began to pace back and forth, occasionally eyeing Lucrezia with a raised brow. Lucrezia however, looked her in the eyes with each time she passed her. Stowe, on the other hand, kept watching over the two like some sort of hawk. Unfortunately, Ariane took swift notice.

"Ease up, boy," she barked. "You're making my ex-husband look like a damn lion with how much I see you shaking in your boots."

Ariane turned her attention back to Lucrezia, waving what objections Stowe had been attempting to make in those moments before turning back to her silent conversation. Lucrezia could see Stowe watching her from the corner of her eye, waiting for something to go wrong or a moment where he would likely need to step in. Yet the moment never came.

"Tell me, little one…" Ariane directs to Lu. "Do the two of you have a destination in mind?"

Come to think of it, Stowe never said anything about where they would be settling. If anything, it was nondescript and left undiscussed.

"I suppose my master and I would have found a place that we found the most comfortable or familiar and wound up settling there."

"So if your *master* led you off of a cliff, would you follow him?"

"To be fair, ma'am, if my master led me off of a cliff, I would be saving his ass."

"LUCREZIA ATHENA MARKOVA!"

Lucrezia and Ariane turned and shot Stowe a dangerous look, forcing the man to freeze in his tracks. He had never seen Lucrezia throw such daggers in the way she had, yet proceeded to remain as still as he could be. In his mind he had hoped that no one else would stop by, or that the two women before him wouldn't look down. In general, he hadn't been quite so sure how to process the situation. He reeled back, containing his shock at the little vampire girl for speaking so... well speaking so outwardly to a damn fae queen.

Ariane, on the other hand, smiled warmly as she slowly bowed to Lu in earnest.

"A pleasure, Miss Markova. Please do keep the stupid boy in line during your stay." She whipped around and glared at Stowe. "As for you, Alexandru..." She continued. "Your new post is going to be along the East Coast where I can keep a bloody eye on you. I'll make sure you have a place to stay for the night, but for your sake, you are to take what is offered and stay where I want you."

Stowe, to his dismay, could not say no.

As the months passed and seasons changed, many things changed. Lucrezia and Stowe's identities remained the same and one challenge after another had been met in stride. The house that they shared, had been assigned to both of them by request. Lu would make meals for Stowe and then go hunting around night fall. They both shared equal responsibility around their new home and took on arrest both together and separately. It was, if anything, almost similar to the life they had when living apart in Seattle. But neither complained. For Stowe, it was nice to come home to someone who would smile up at him and ask about his day. For Lucrezia, it was nice to have someone who respected her boundaries and genuinely cared about whether or not she had felt safe.

However....

Things seemed to change when they had hit their year mark. The two were sent to patrol the docks of Brooklyn out of suspicion that there may be some breach of treaty between the local solitary groups. And while the two waited, they began to play a game. The game had started off innocent at first, and as time went on things began to grow more and more intense. Before they knew it, Stowe had Lucrezia pinned beneath him, giggling softly as he grinned triumphantly at his victory. His eyes then went to her lips as the giggling slowed to a halt and he found that she had been gazing up at him. Daring him to make a move. Her fingers trickled along his arm and paused at his shoulder as she bit her lower lip. She leaned up and brushed her lips against his, testing the waters and pulling back to see if her master would reciprocate. He paused, thinking for a moment as he moved forward and caught her chin between his thumb and forefinger, pressing his lips to hers as the smell of earth and peonies filled his senses. He could feel her fingers clutch at the front of his shirt as he pressed forward and struggled to discard his jacket. Her legs intertwined with his as she whimpered with need and he reached for the lever at the side of the passenger seat to press her back further. They both remained unsure of whether or not this was a passing fantasy, yet neither truly cared at that moment. But the moment Stowe felt the jingling of his belt, everything skid to a halt. He tore himself back and found himself panting and gasping for air. She was looking up at him with surprise and wondering what she had done.

Did he not want her? She wondered.

Stowe could see her processing the situation and nodding, almost in acceptance as hurt and disappointment slowly built a wall between the two. And he mentally began to beat himself up over the endeavor.

Once the assignment had been said and done, she avoided him. She hid in her room and covered herself more often. She only said a few words to him, despite his efforts of starting a conversation. He felt as though he gave off the wrong impression by pulling away.

The time wasn't right.

The setting wasn't ideal.

She deserved a better situation.

Stowe began to place flowers at her bedroom door. Leave her sweet notes that portrayed his thoughts of her. Soon after she began to write him letters, sliding under his door. They would eventually go on walks and talk about nothing or everything. And sometimes, they wouldn't talk about anything at all.

"Do you see us together for a while?" he asked her early one morning.

"I never really believed in forever, Stowe," she responded.

Stowe scoffed and rolled his eyes as he then flicked a cheerio in Lucrezia's direction. "I never said forever, doll," he retorted.

"I said a while."

"Maybe till you're old and your jaw falls off."

The Nephilim gave a suggestive grin as he scooted forward, leaning into her ear as if others were listening in on their conversation.

"Then I guess I should make some good use of it until then, shouldn't I?"

Lucrezia could feel as Stowe's fingers curled around her hand and pulled her from her seat atop the kitchen counter. Her eyes filled with wonder as he led her up the stairs and down their hallway, pulling her into his room before closing the door behind her. He pressed her against the door and stopped her other hand from reaching for the light switch with his. His golden green eyes fixed on her violets, holding her there as he leaned in for a kiss. He ensured that she would remain pinned against the door, unable to escape him as he lifted her by the buttocks, never once breaking the kiss as he wrapped her legs around his waist. He could feel himself harden as she pulled herself closer, wrapping her arms around his shoulders as he laid her down upon his bed. His fingers danced along her sides and squeezed at her hips as his lips left hers, moving down to her collar bone and biting as hard as she could manage.

Mine. He thought to himself. *All mine, for however long she wants me.*

Stowe began to remove what garments he could as he left a trail of butterfly kisses from her clavicle to her navel, never daring to stop until he had managed to reach his prize, and oh, he was determined that he would.

He could feel her fist at his hair in anticipation as he tugged at the waistband of her shorts, enjoying how she writhed beneath him, whining and pleading for him to continue.

"Stowe, please…" she mewled. "Please continue."

Suddenly, a dark thought came to mind. "Whatever happened to *Master*?"

"Call me Kitten, and I just might."

Stowe rose to a sitting position and gave a soft sigh.

"I'm sorry, I forgot to ask." He moved to a standing position, walking to his nightstand and withdrawing a leather collar with a gold heart shaped padlock. Confused, Lucrezia sat up and turned to face him.

"Would you, Lucrezia Markova, be my Kitten for as long as you see fit?"

Trial, Error, and a Cat on My Keyboard with Nothing to do with Said Cat

There are many things that transpired between the pages of my youth. Now that I am twenty seven, I look back and wonder what could have changed and scour through the memories and experiences that I now have to live with.

When we are young, we make mistakes. And like surfing, we either ride the wave and turn with the tide, or we swim away from it and fall off of our board. Sometimes we even ride the wave and fall off of our boards. I laugh to myself as I think of the concussion that followed suit with that event, and how it disqualified me from surfing soon after. I would still go into the water. I would still try, but in the end, I would find that I wasn't really cut out for it. Life has a funny way of telling you whether or not you're meant for something and I guess the teenager that was me really could not take a hint.

I've changed a lot since then.

I no longer have an interest in surfing or doing any sports of the like. I have more of an interest in acting and film. Writing is a thing that allows me to delve into the depths of my strange imagination and share it with the world. It allows me to face reality and pick and choose what it is that I want to share versus things that I would love to keep as a dirty little secret. And honestly, I find no shame in it. It is a career of humility mixed in with a personal self-fulfillment that I may or may not have had since I was a child.

I remember collaborating stories with my grandmother as she helped me with my writing. We would start with three word sentences and add on to them, one after the other. Soon the sentences would go from three words to four and so on. I would have fun writing with her. She and I would keep a personal journal between the two of us and she would call them the Ayakashi Adventures Volume x. She would sometimes include new words for me to learn, and once I had understood, she would encourage me to read them to her. To further build my confidence, she would have me write a short story and bring it in to class for show and tell, hoping that it would build my confidence. This, however, became more and more difficult after she died. My stories became more and more horrific, I was met with a depression that I hadn't been sure that anyone could possibly understand. And one night, I heard my mother and father fighting. I could hear their screams getting louder and louder and all I could think of was the warpath that would be left behind. I began to write about the Gashadokuro, the bone giant, that would manifest during great times of starvation or in battlefields filled with unburied dead. I then added the Oni-baba, the hag and Jorogumo-Hime, Lady Spider and wrote and wrote about how all would chase after a crane, a fox and a ningyo for their own selfish desires. The crane would represent loyalty and servitude, the fox would represent luck and the ningyo— known to most as a mermaid- would represent eternal youth and immortality. Gashadokuro, Oni-baba and Jorogumo-Hime would all be seen as parental figures to the three main characters. All three antagonists would be loved by the three afformentioned characters, but would be consumed by greed. Just as my parents were. Just as any one of my aunts or uncles on my mothers side would be, and to me, it had been a fate that I would be forced to accept. And nothing was more liberating to me than becoming the black sheep.

"You're a good girl, you would never do bad." I would always hear. "All I need is a foot rub, but after you get me a drink."

In my mothers family, if you are a child, you are an indentured servant until death. If you complain or want to do something else, you are seen as ungrateful. I would get things thrown at me or hit.

Needless to say, I was never the golden child. I was kida to few and that in and of its self was hardly a blessing. There was a matron who was referred to as Auntie Bennett. She would be kind depending on who you spoke to, but under the surface she was very catholic. I remember very little of her, yet the few memories that I do have of her are… fuzzy to say the least. My late grandfather, however, was a very strict man. He was one of the few people who my mother had been afraid of, and even then, he hid the reason for that fear away from me. What I remember of him is little more than the dreams of a small child. When we spent time together, he would play the saxophone and have me sing, we would sing along to popular movies that he'd brought home and he would barbeque chicken or fish while red rice was cooking. To me, he was a very gentle and kind person who would tell me stories of how he and his brothers would get into trouble during the fifties. Life on Guam before the technological era was never really what one would call exciting. If anything it was a secondary paradise for lonely old soldiers to visit and find an exotic wife to settle down with outside of the US. Or if you were anything like grandpa Phillip, play Chamorro dukes of hazard with said lonely old soldiers. Having seen the original dukes of hazard, the comparison is not too far off from what grandpa Phillip did. But thankfully, instead of the confederate flag, it was the Guam flag that would be printed upon the hood of his truck. I know, because there are pictures of that damn truck next to a younger version of my mother in eighties booty shorts. Though, it's memories of my grandfather like that that make me miss him as I move forward to the constant contradictions of my dreams being invalidated. My dreams of being an actor, my dreams of writing stories for everyone to see and the weight of pressure I had undergone with narcissistic parents.

I had the good people in my life, yes.

But there were more bad than good. And constantly I wonder if it is even ok to set an inkling of blame for my life as it is today. I'm often told that a person is responsible to how unexpected situations are handled. If that were the case, then the unexpected situations that befell me and mine would have turned positive in an instant. If that were true, I wouldn't feel suicidal every time I tried to face the causes of my PTSD. I wouldn't hear my mother, father, aunts and uncles in my head screaming at me for how worthless I am, how I can't be better or how others despise me simply for the fact that I exist. And I wouldn't be scared to reach out and discuss how difficult it is to try and live through every god damn day, trying to keep myself off of autopilot. Trying not to disassociate, trying to be present for those who genuinely want me.

I worry every day for my writing and acting career. I worry that I won't be good enough and even feign confidence that I am the best at what I do before going home and breaking down.

Talk about it?

With whom?

As far as experience goes, unless there is a genuine interest, I remain unsure of who I can go to. To describe it, my head is a plane and my comfort is piloting it. Seldom do I find myself capable of moving freely throughout the cabin. And when I do, the words "within reason" play through my head.

Because of my parents, there is no such thing as "moving freely". Because of my abusers, safe isn't in my vocabulary. And now, I am finding that there was a lot that I repressed growing up. I worry about expressing too much anger. I'm afraid of showing too much emotion. I'm terrified of being too sedate. All because negative emotions are "unattractive" and sedate means that "I don't care".

There are nights where I just sit up and stare into the darkness, searching for the endless void that I used to fear so much. On occasion the snores from my pets and my partners draws my attention away from any invasive thoughts that me enter, distracting me from reminiscing of a time where it wasn't quiet. And for that, my only thoughts are of whether I will get to sleep that night or how much I envy either for sleeping so well. I will admit that I am glad to have them in my life. Their presence brings me joy. But still, there is the underlying fear that they will grow bored of me, and eventually run as far away as they can. And I am terrified. I shut down, feeling as though the possibility awaits me from just around the corner. And were I to make that one wrong move, my life as I know it would set the ground to crumble beneath my feet and the vast forest of temporary solace ablaze. To which belies the question of whether or not I will ever find peace. Will I betray my children in to a state of constant fear as I have been? Will they see me in the same light as I see my parents, or will I be better?

As I look at it, I am unsure.

I don't know if I will ever truly live for that long.

If I don't, I pray that no one will think of me to follow.

If I do, I'm not quite sure.

I always worry about whether or not my mental health issues will pass on to my children. It is a future that I can neither foresee, nor prevent if it does happen. I don't even know if I will make it that far.

But really, all I can provide is that I am trying. I am doing my best to live from day to day with what I am capable of expending, just so I can see my career through. It's not easy. It will never be easy, and certainly no walk in the park.

And my dear reader, if you have made it this far with my dribble just know...

There are people in this world who thrive on hurting you and chances are, you are much stronger than me. Chances are, you will only have to deal with one and manage to stay away from them. Or you are like me, and somehow manage to attract them. You may have very recently had a friend who robbed you of your choices, as I've had. You may even feel as though you are at fault. And if you do, I would like you to know that you carry no blame. The bad things that others have done to you are the actions of the antagonist, not to you. Do not take the blame for someone elses shitty actions, as they do not deserve it. They do not deserve what energy you have already given them. They lost that privilege the moment they decided to hurt you. And hopefully you have someone kind, someone who is loving and someone who is understanding to help you the rest of the way. Because you, my dear reader are deserving of it.

There are good people who love you. People who will cherish you and give you the care that you deserve. And sometimes, they are gone as soon as they arrive.

I had a friend like that.

I keep her in my heart.

I keep her in my memories.

She will always be a sister to me.

You likely have that too.

I am not writing this as a word of warning. I think about the amount of times I was betrayed and this story was probably one of the more difficult stories for me to write. Because when all your looking for is the bad, that is all you're going to focus on. That is all you're going to find. It becomes an obsession that you can never get over and it slowly falls over you like hot tar, eating you alive bit by bit. And it will be nothing other than the pain it was meant to cause. But when you aren't paying attention, when you're neither looking for the good nor the bad, both somehow manage to jump out and surprise you. Both may even be seen as a lesson or a blessing. Of course, there are things in this world that somehow let you know whether or not you are on the right path in some way or another, one just needs to know how and where to look, as wishy washy as that may sound.

Needless to say, my life has had a lot of bad and I have done things I am not proud of. Right now, it just feels as though I am at a stand still and it's so peaceful that I am afraid that the entire world may be against me. I am afraid that I will no longer be wanted among certain groups or if my existence would even be considered valid by this point. It's an odd state to be in. On one hand, I am a professional writer for a wonderful organization who has managed to put up with my nonsense this far along. On the other, I find that I am missing the rainy and cold state of Washington while looking for more and more ways to keep myself alive and trying to work toward a bigger and brighter future.

But as I said, I am healing.

It's a long and messy process that no one should have to go through, despite many having to. It takes energy, it takes work. And the worse part is that you never know how many obstacles you will encounter in the week. To some, there are few and to others, there are too many to count. One of my partners constantly undergoes more hell that she deserves at her work. She deals with a lot of self loathing due to her chronic pain and disabilities, and some days, the most one can do is be there and try to help where one is able. My other partner has dysphoria and chronic depression that makes it difficult for him to get out of bed. And then there is my third who has chronic depression and anxiety that he seldom leaves his room. And I am thankful for all three. I love all of them for how wonderful they are and they have become part of a list of blessings that a younger me could never imagine.

As hard as my life is, as deep as my trauma goes, I am trying.

I am trying to make a life that is mine.

I am trying to stay present.

I am doing what I can.

And my dear reader, if you are healing, you have my pride. It's a long road. But if you made it this far, I am proud of you. I look forward to the day where you are successful.

THE RESCUE

Chapter 1

Tick. Tock. Tick. Tock.

Those infernal seconds of silence never settled well with her. Why would they? When one is locked in a dark room all alone, left beside themselves for however many years without a soul to talk to, the once endearing sound of a clock becomes the bane of one's existence. At first, the sound was reminiscent of a music beat. The songs that she would formulate would have even tempos that were slow and melodious as they paced well with the clock. She often imagined the gears and pistons working in unison as an intermachinal ballet of dancers, moving with precision and well-practiced choreography. Yet the inner workings of the clock in the hall way also added a rhythm of their own, syncing to the beat of her songs. However, she grew bored and they all began to sound the same. When one tires of tempos and music, it is difficult to find a remedy to ever obtain the joys of that stage of the art back. This left only stories and a convoluted imaginary theater that she would play for herself. There would be a show every night with a grand party of one as she would tell herself and play stories of the classics. Persephone's descent into the underworld, the Shakespeare's Much Ado About Nothing, as well as notorious historic events, whether they be good or bad. She would likely be the few to admit that Gaius Augustus Caesar was an interesting fellow with bright ideas, but the wrong party to help carry it out and she supposed he became some odd form of inspiration for swiss cheese somewhere down the line. However, these stories were not to say that she lacked imagination. In fact some of the stories she came up with or formulated in her head sometimes kept her up at night. But even that joy began to fade as the music had. She no longer held interest of an unsung protagonist stuck in endless loops. That was where she knew that she was running out of any and all creative ideas. She eventually resorted to memorizations and counting games. When does the doctor come? When does she next get her drug meal? When does she get her actual meal?

What?

The doctors didn't really expect her not to know that they were drugging her cranberry sausage oatmeal with brown sugar and butter, did they? It was likely why they now avoid adding pepper.

Tick.

Tock.

Tick.

Tock.

She wondered how long it would take for her patience to wear thin. The ticking had already become needless.

How long till one goes mad?

Or had she already gone mad?

And if she had already gone mad, when and whereabouts did she lose her sanity?

She leaned back against the wall and closed her eyes,

picturing an endless sea of stars and a bright cool blue light as she drifted along. She pictured beautiful creatures much like blue whales drifting along with her as they glided together in pods, nearly blinding passers by with their unexpected bioluminescence. She moved to reach out and touch one as it moved beside her, yet was taken from the fantasy as she instantly fell on her side and strained against the bindings of her straight jacket. Her bliss was now gone.

She scowled and shifted in her added confines as she sat herself upright again. She wasn't ready for sleep, despite it being as dark as it was.

Constance, she whispered to herself. She thought that was her name.

The doctors put her down as Constance Smith, as she had no means of identification or pay. She could only tell them that her name was Constance.

From then on, one doctor after another would ask her question after question regarding things she couldn't begin to answer. Things she hadn't been so sure she had even had to begin with. And no matter how much she tried to remember, she would continue to draw a blank. She wouldn't deny that she would sometimes fall into a mild obsession and ruminate to a point where her incarceration may have seemed necessary for others. She liked to imagine a childhood from time to time, and yet she couldn't bring herself to tell a lie. She often questioned how it was possible for one to forget being a child. To even forget aspects of their life that could perhaps help them escape their present situation had proven to be no less than ludicrous. In fact it had been part of the reason why Constance had been given the wonderful cocktailed diagnoses of Melancholia with a side of amnesia salted atop a healthy serving of pseudo psychosis.

And the drugs only made her worse.

There had been times where she would fall into a screaming frenzy without sedation, men in white would flood into her cell and hold her down until she was calm. One of the doctors once suggested a transorbital lobotomy. Luckily the other doctors protested against it. These instances were times where she would wake up scared, shaking, screaming in a language with origins neither she nor any of the sanitorium staff could place.

She couldn't help but wonder what she looked like during these instances or after. The cell they had placed her in had been a darkened padded cell in the east wing, and likely the oldest in the building. The fire proof tin door had a flap where they would insert treys of food. And most of the time she hardly needed the straight jacket. Unfortunately, the nearest window had been too high for her to reach. Yet she still daydreamed of the day when she would feel the warmth of the sun on her face with the sounds of birds chittering in her ears. Places like these lacked such luxuries.

Such places, it seemed, were always void of life.

"My, how the mighty have fallen," came a voice.

All it took for the voice's owner to appear was a slow blink.

A wolf skull bore down upon Constance as she peered up with intrigue. Stag horns protruded from a tattered black shroud as the same material pooled around the figure in an inky black mound. Sigils had been etched into the skull for reasons that Constance couldn't fathom. What's more, she wondered why the figure had entered with an age old phrase.

"That's a pretty impressive costume," she complimented. "I didn't think Halloween would be around for another year or so."

A clawed hand shot out from the mess of black fabric and pressed her back against the wall. Their fingers curled around her neck. Fiery red embers glowed within the sockets and leered down upon the unsuspecting inpatient. And looking at the figure, Constance found herself in a state of internal conflict.

"Do you not remember me?"

The figures voice was low and gravelly, yet surprisingly calm for one who had just wrapped their expensive manicured hand around the throat of a complete stranger. She would remember meeting a shrouded figure within or outside of the confines of her wild imagination, who—if they were on a date—would very likely wave some pretty large red flags.

"Honestly, I don't think I would want to, buddy."

The fingers curled tighter around her throat, threatening to cut off her air ways.

"I am the keeper of the void," the figure said. "I rule all of that which is in the shadows and call forth the most horrific of nightmares."

"I still don't know or want to know you."

"Whether you like it or not, you will learn soon, little muse." Within the blink of an eye, the figure had disappeared. No warning. No say as to who he was. No relevancy to his entrance or his approach.

So, like many things irrelevant, Constance simply brushed it off to the back of her mind.

The next morning did not come with the drugged breakfast she had grown used to and her time in the straight jacket had come to an end. Nurses flooded in and out of her cell this time to ensure that her vitals were regular, and yet she still couldn't chase the reason as to why.

At least, that was until a man stepped through the doorway with a clip board tucked beneath his arm. Needless to say that he wasn't her usual fare. He didn't stuff himself into a lab coat like the others and he seemed to enjoy wearing a red sweater over a blue collar button up shirt with a black tie and his kakis were stained with blue and black ink where he tried to wipe evidence of a leaky pen off of his hands.

"Good morning Miss Smith," the good doctor greeted with a soft tone.

"I am Bartolomeu Void, and starting today, I will be your new primary care provider."

Something was off about this one. She couldn't fathom as to why, but something about this particular doctor set her hairs on edge. Could it have been that he wasn't who he said he was? Could it be that he was the figure from last night and thought that she couldn't tell? Who else did he think he was fooling with a name like Bartolomeu Void? So now the creature who visited her dons a Mr. Rogers getup with curly chestnut hair and freckles with brilliant green hazel eyes and he thinks that she is instantly fooled?

"For how long?" she asked.

"For as long as it takes to get you on your feet."

There were many things that were going through Constance's head in that moment. One being that she could easily stand on her own and the other where she wanted to ask where she was being taken. The doctor paced around her slowly, looking her up and down and going back to her charts as she coughed. Part of her was certain that she did not like where this was going and she was beginning to feel a little uncomfortable with the ordeal.

"But first, I would prefer a more up to date room among other inmates."

Or not.

"In a more medically approved facility focused on the health and well being of it's patients."

Now she was confused.

Chapter 2

The departure from the hospital was nothing short of uneventful, and frankly, the smell of the facility had made Constance a little light headed as her first breath of fresh air nearly sent her falling into an unexpected wave of euphoria as the warmth of the suns rays poured down upon her face and she couldn't help but close her eyes. For the first time in a while she could feel herself slip into a state of momentary bliss. Her fingers stretched out and she could feel her body loosen up for the first time.

Freedom.

She wondered just how long she had been in the sanitorium. She was curious how many years it had been since she was taken in and was therefore unsurprised when the answer came to be three years.

"I suppose that's the reason why it felt so long."

"Well it's not like you didn't have anything there to entertain you was it?"

There was a long pause as Doctor Void waited patiently for her answer.

"Surely they didn't keep you in an outdated and heavily infested part of the building, did they?"

Constance laughed. It was that bad was it?

"I honestly didn't mind the spiders."

"As a mental health and care facility, they should have provided a better means of care over a rundown part of the building."

Should they have? She didn't know.

"Honestly, I am close to filing a complaint with the state and showing you the process of how to press charges. The conditions they had you in were ridiculous."

"Are you saying that because you mean it or are you saying that because you love the sound of your own voice?"

"Both."

The level of surprised silence sent a long pause through Doctor Voids car. Neither knew what else to say to one and other and often times the stops were quick and only for the allotted amount of snacks that could be afforded. Beyond that any conversations were walled off and let alone to their own devices and it wasn't until they had reached a clearing beneath a bridge that either of them said a word.

"Where are we headed?" Constance asked.

"A small sanctuary near the original Jamestown settlement."

Constance hadn't been sure how to approach the answer as she leaned further into her chair.

"I noticed that you haven't looked at yourself in the mirror."

She had forgotten that she was allowed to look in the mirror, now and was somewhat afraid of her appearance.

"Afraid of how you might look?"

"No."

"Prove it."

She looked over to Bartolomeu and quirked a brow before laughing and sighing.

"I figured."

Bartolomeu Void looked over at her with a pointed gaze and scoffed. He knew what she had caught onto and was hardly surprised, given her reaction to him in the sanitorium. Why shouldn't she say anything or make any remarks about it now.

"You're the guy who came to my cell last night."

He did not expect that.

In fact, he had never even met her until this morning after spending months to prepare a retrieval for her. But really he wondered exactly what she was talking about when it came to someone visiting her in that damp old cell.

"I never met you until this morning."

He could see her face drop in confusion, and pulled to a halt before stepping out of the vehicle. And he could tell that she was watching his every move from then on as he paced back and forth, spinning around in circles before inhaling and exhaling. She couldn't have been visited by him, could she? Did she even know what she was or have any inkling as to why he came to retrieve her to begin with? He hopped back in the care and settled in the drivers seat as he closed his eyes and pinched the bridge of his nose, unsure what to make of it.

"Constance, how did you get in to the asylum?"

Constance sighed and shrugged.

"All I can remember is a bright light and waking up on a highway with no clothes and no idea who I was or even my name. There was a dead trucker in a crashed sixteen wheeler off the side of the road whose flesh was practically melting from the bone and a nametag on the uniform that said Constance. I liked the name, so I took it."

"And how did you end up at the sanitorium?"

"Easy, I walked into the nearest town naked and said *HELLO WORLD, MY NAME IS CONSTANCE*, to which nobody minded, but I digress. And it was a small town called Copperville and had mostly been abandoned for a really long time, save for the few people who were left in some of the crumbling houses, there."

"Can they vouch for you?"

"I think they're dead at this point. It was a little over thirty years ago and the whole *don't run around naked* thing wasn't as big of a deal until maybe three years ago when I had entered I think the Williamsburg library?"

"So you've been running around naked for thirty years?"

"Yes."

"Look in the damn mirror."

She sighed and looked over to the rear view mirror, spying an ivory skinned woman with silver hair and bright blue eyes. The woman's lips settled into a pout as she slowly looked back to her companion with a low laugh and a feeling of bewilderment.

"And here I thought I had black hair."

Bartolomeu nodded.

"I had heard about you being caught naked in a library from your medical records," he said. "They were originally going to arrest you for public indecency before they found out that you honestly had little to no idea that what you were doing was... well."

"So tell me something."

"Yes?"

"Are you really a doctor?"

That one, Bartolomeu was not going to answer. Instead he smiled and continued to drive. Saying nothing more of the matter as he continued onward, moving through the brush of tree's as night began to fall. He knew that he was likely never going to figure out who the shrouded man was. He knew that there were supernatural beings who were in need of being taken out of harsh situations like Constance's. Beings like Constance who had long forgotten who they were, save for a few pleasant memories and a hat trick here and there. Either way, he was excited to see where the road would take him with this crazy woman if she so decided to stay. But alas, that was her choice and hers alone.

Kill Ticket

ecilia Meyers drove along the coast line with the windows down. The ocean breeze swayed through her ebony hair as the smell of brine filled her senses. For at least a moment, she could consider her options. She could consider more honorable paths that didn't involve her needing to spill blood or possibly having her blood spilled if she stepped out of line. And in all honesty, she had been in a desperate situation when she had first joined the mafia. Sure she knew what that sort of thing meant. She had even considered the risks and the consequences when she had so much as decided that she no longer wanted to starve. And not even fast food places had been hiring at the time, especially for people on the streets. And surely no one would want someone jobless moving in without *proper* means of payment. She was too prideful for that sort of thing.

Most nights she would go about her business without a hitch. She loved that. She loved not having to attend to the beck and call of her boss, loved not staining her hands with any more blood than she was ordered. The ability to roam free had enticed her beyond belief. And dancing as though no one had been watching or preparing to kill her on sight had called to her more than once. However, it was often nights like these ones, where the illusion of choice and freedom, had been little more than sickeningly sweet dreams. Gone was the humanity of a hit man, who as a grunt bore little to no importance or footing. When told to jump, Cecilia was to respond with "How high?" And when men like her boss, when men like Marco pointed at a target, the option to say no was dangerous. Family stopped being family. Friends were no longer friends. If a person went so far as to anger Marco to land on his black list, however deep the rabbit hole had gone dependent on how terrible the offense... whether or not the act of offended were petty or not.

When this happened, no one was safe.

She merged into the next lane and turned in to the nearest exit, crossing the Golden Gate Bridge just moments later. Thanking the travel time to allow her to turn her emotions off, to the rest of the world and prepare herself for the scene she would soon walk in to.

His new catch of the day mewled and writhed beneath him as he had bent her over the table, thrusting in a flurry of anger and frustration at how submissive the bitch had been. He despised how she begged for his attention and practically chased him to and fro about the office. Next he would hear about how he got her pregnant and demand repentance.

He hated women like this one. He hated how much they would beg for him to get to his money and hated that they pined after him. He hated easy targets and often wished that killing them on sight wouldn't expose his underworld activities. Expensive prostitutes were untrustworthy. His assistants were far too uppity to bother with him unless it involved scheduling a meeting and ensuring that his meetings went along smoothly. Honestly, he despised them almost as much as the easy little harlots who flitted after him.

"Come in," he growled as a knock came to the door.

His thrusts grew more and more violent as the woman beneath him cried out. Her nails dug in to the paper schedule atop his desk, protecting the cherry oak beneath as yet another woman entered his office. Her expression was cold and off putting as she slowly closed the door and waited for his completion in silence. He gave her a cocky grin as he felt a mild wash of lust fall over him. Her silver eyes were unmoved by his antics, and if anything the air of disgust that she tried to hide from him only managed to turn him on even more.

"I didn't think you would be here so soon," he huffed. "I've always liked that about you, Morpho."

The way her lips formed into a pout as she tried her best to remain unshaken from his statement had been rather adorable. He lived for subjecting her to any form of mental and emotional torment as he saw fit when she met alone with him, and never bothered with hesitation. He could see her muscles tense and contort as discomfort overcame her and the idea of the woman beneath him... he stopped his thoughts as only the thought of finishing crossed his mind. He proceeded to grab his latest catch by the hair and continued to batter her from just over his desk.

"Tell Morpho she's beautiful," he commanded.

The woman let out a low murmur, whimpering a protest as she grit her teeth.

Marco slowed to a halt and the woman nearly cried out, begging him to continue. There was a displeased expression on his face as he glared down at her.

"I see."

The woman turned around to face him, opening her mouth to argue right as he pinned her back down by the throat.

"You know, I really fucking hate women like you," he chided. His fingers squeezed harder as he felt her attempting to fight him.

"You come to work for my company, suspecting nothing, following orders until the situation suits you best, and then you fucking turn around and disobey."

Cecilia shuddered at the venomous edge in his voice. He had intended to kill the woman beneath him and it scared her for the reason he would do it.

"And not only do you disobey, you insult my woman."

She had to remain calm at this moment. Any reaction could mean her life. She cared little for how he was treating another life and wanted little to do with the fact. She had to turn a blind eye. She had to ensure that she stayed safe above all else and could not risk her life for someone else's over being treated as though she were the product of some sick mans fantasy. She couldn't object. But she could, in the very least collect a payout to deliver. Some sort of settlement to which could set her free, she hoped.

A loud snapping sound echoed through the room and caught Cecilia's attention. The woman that had been enjoying herself on her bosses desk now lay dead with her head faced down. The psychopath who had killed her merely adjusted and straightened himself out as though what he had done were meaningless. But... she drew herself in. Wasn't this always how he had been with her? Always doing something to get a rise? Always trying to get a reaction out of her to prove how soft she was and to remind her that at the end of the day, she was always nothing more than a woman to him? She held her tongue as he continued to straighten himself out and brush the dead woman off the desk. His eyes were, if anything, cold and unfeeling.

"Now..." he began. "I'm sure you know why I've summoned you here?"

The sudden change in his moods had scared her. And the very idea that he was of the more mercurial sort would send a chill down anyone's spine.

"Actually sir, I was hoping you would tell me?"

Marco paused, sneering over at her as if questioning him were going to be the last thing she had ever done. His gold eyes fixed on her, eyeing her up and down as he tried to make a move before her. Yet found nothing of interest.

"I called you here to talk to you about your younger sister."

Finally, she had lost control and gave him a reaction. What had her sister done to warrant Marco's attention? What could Cecilia do to get her out of the situation? Did she have to kill her?

The mafia boss smiled at her, as if she had given him something he wanted.

"Amelie has wracked up quite a debt with the company, and it's become a bit of a bother."

She didn't like where this is going.

"I need you to take her out for me."

This was one thing she had hoped she would never have to do.

Finding a replacement had been a difficult endeavor to say the least. The decoy had proven to be quite resistant in their procurement. But Cecilia wondered when her targets had ever been easy. So as she paced back and forth while the young woman of perhaps nineteen or twenty swayed her head to and fro. With how long the girl had been out, it had been no surprise that she would soon begin to panic. Finding herself in a dimly lit room with nothing more than a swinging light and the sound of footsteps tapping in tune with distant dripping and splashing noises. She wouldn't be able to move much beyond twisting and writing within her binds. And if she tried to scream, she would only run out of energy and ware down to a panting and writhing mess.

In fact, that is exactly what the young girl had done as Cecilia remained in the shadows. Not responding to her targets protests and bargains.

Sounds like internal or external pandemonium had always managed to trigger some sort of animalistic instinct within Cecilia. As if prolonging the targets inevitable demise would somehow make the kill sweeter, more purposeful on both parts. And she often wondered if that instinct had been something she had been born with or if it had been learned.

"Please," the young girl begged.

"Please, don't kill me, I will do anything."

Anything? No. No, no no. That won't do. Anything is for those who have freedom to move around without fear or repercussions. Anything is for those who have done nothing to warrant being killed or getting anyone else killed. And the poor girl just happened to be one of the unlucky ones to obtain someone else's kill ticket.

Cecilia would work toward amends to her family once she managed to leave her predicament, but for now… for now, she had at least one final job to do.

Once Cecilia had found she had had enough she began to get to work. She started with removing one of her victims fingers. Slowly tearing the skin from the knuckle as she imbibed in the act of torture. Her heart leaped with sadistic frenzy as the younger being screamed in both terror and agony. No one could hear her. No one would come for her. Just as no one had heard or come for Cecilia. Why should this unlucky target of a black lottery be any different? And she rather enjoyed the trepidation of those who fell beneath her knife. And the more that the girl screamed, the more joy she felt. Yet her face would remain blank, still and unfeeling. She wouldn't want the poor dear to know how much she liked the girls slow and methodical torment, it would make her lose hope.

No.

She couldn't allow that.

Instead, she proceeded to break her targets fingers and look in her eyes as she decided she had grown weary of her screams. The girls lips were then sewn shut with little regard and she couldn't vocally express her agony as it came. Hours would soon pass as the flow of time took its course. The girl had eventually succumbed to a brain aneurysm. Cecilia guessed that such extended torture had proven too much. Still, it was pretty impressive that she had managed to survive as long as she had. Her murderer acknowledged that much.

Still, she wondered what the girl could have achieved with that kind of will power. She wondered what sort of life could have been achieved in what life she had had left.

Either way, it was her younger sister who dug this girls grave. Cecilia remained responsible for the clean up and went into another room three walls over, where a mattress with moss and overgrowth lay bent over a pitch black trash bag. Peaks of green could be seen through the stretched out plastic, yet not for reasons one would think. The old building that the hit man had tended to her work had officially been set ablaze with no signs of a corpse. Cecilia's clothes had been changed and then burned within the dumpster nearby. The finger had been placed in a Zale's box along with a ring and fancy wrapping. Her heart feeling the tinge of what was to come.

She had been gone for hours, he thought to himself. He had so hoped that she had quickly done the deed so to get it over with, and just bring him proof of her sisters death. Yet she had proven just how stone hearted she could be. Which is why he liked her so much. He wanted her attention on him. He wanted her to obey him and show him some iota of warmth on a cold day. He would lovingly bend her over any desk or surface she would allow him. He danced for the idea of her falling to her knees after wearing her down. And god, he lived for the idea of her. She was a good girl.

She was his good girl.

She just didn't know it yet.

His office doors swung open and she entered the room with stride. There was a look of defiance on her face as she approached his desk with a briefcase in one hand, and a zales jewelry box in another. He leaned back and watched her with subtle praise as she sat in front of him. She walked with some form of newfound confidence for some reason or another, which as odd as it was, had been nothing short of attractive. She set the brief case on his desk and then placed the zales box right next to it. He reached for the box and opened it slowly, finding a freshly cut finger with a gold band on it. It seemed she had done the job with gusto.

"Morpho, baby..." he crooned. "You're too much."

"Don't call me baby."

Marco looked up in shock at his interest as she stared down her nose at him. The sheer expression of disgust toward him had been enough to make him want to strike her. What right did she have to talk to him like that? His boss? She was lucky that he liked her enough to remain silent for a brief moment as he thought about her words.

"Should I call you a dog then?" he half joked.

"Because only bitches give orders."

Now his Morpho's expression grew cocky. Perhaps because of what the suitcase contained?

"You're not to call me anything, Marco," she said to him. "I'm leaving and I'm turning my life around."

She could feel the air thicken around the room as his eyes filled with fire. His hands slammed down on the desk as he quickly rose and reached out to her.

"I could give you anything," he growled at her.

"You could have the fucking world if you wanted."

She looked to the briefcase and sighed. Marco seemed to think that she belonged to him beyond just working for him.

"There is enough in that briefcase to pay off my cut."

Her eyes narrowed at the overgrown man child as her stomach filled with disgust. She wanted nothing to do with him, let alone be in the same room with him. Yet here he was, enjoying himself with his late fathers mediocre empire. She wondered what he did to earn it, what work he put in after lazing around all day and night and sipping cocktails like some millionaire playboy from the projects. Were he to grow up with nothing, were he to have been cut off and penniless, women like her would eat him alive and dump him in the streets with the skin off his bones.

Cecilia could feel the sadistic frenzy tickle at the back of her shoulder as she smiled at him. The mans shitty way of begging was enough to make her laugh, and she almost couldn't believe how long she had allowed him control over her. Instead she turned her back on him and proceeded to walk out.

"*I fucking own you!*" she could hear him shout beyond the door.

Night had fallen and Cecilia had settled in a nearby smoke bar. The smell of cigarettes and clove wafted through the air as she crossed one leg over the other. Soft blues played through the vicinity with a slow and mellow beat cooled her nerves while she took swig after swig of a twelve year scotch. She spied her reflection nearby and smiled. She had never seen herself so relaxed in ten years. She had often found herself tense and looking over her shoulder every five minutes. She just needed that moment. That was all she needed and had been one of the little things she had taken for granted in her youth.

BANG!

Her eyes shot open as she set her glass of scotch down,

looking over the back of her seat as a man exited a vibrant red car outside of the bar window. Another man stormed out and touched his head in frustration. The other man standing beside him touched his shoulder and passed his card over with ease. Likely exchanging insurance information so that he could take care of a situation that he had unwittingly caused.

It wasn't a gunshot.

Cecilia gave a soft sigh of relief.

It wasn't a gun shot.

She went back to lounging in her seat with ease, taking her scotch back up and slowly sipping away at it. She closed her eyes and took in a breath. All was calm. There was no violence for now and her past experiences would one day prove to be a world away.

Ash and Bone

Most often times those who are emotionally unavailable carry themselves away with falling for fictional characters. Sometimes, even the writer falls for their characters or the characters of another person for good measure, so that they may avoid any pain or trespass from a stranger. In years such as 2020, it is just as hard and even as understandable to find ones self becoming emotionally attached to a character that cannot die or has died in a story. However, the thing about stories is that, that is all that they are. And when one is immersed in them, when one consumes the words, the thoughts and feelings that the writer conveys and the emotions that paint the landscapes and universe beneath the readers fingertips it allows an escape from reality. Even if it is just for a moment or hours or even a week. Sometimes it is needed.

I feel that many can agree that it has been an unprecedented year. And many children will vaguely know what birthday parties are like. Many adults and teenagers will never or vaguely understand the intimacy of a first date. Many are distant while others...not so much.

The elections and the blatant disregard for human life have aged many like me. I have watched people I love succumb to illnesses because they could not afford medication and I have broken down and reached out for help. I have lost and fought for energy that I barely had.

Things will never go back to the way they used to be.

Honestly, as a human being, I don't want them to. I want things to move forward, for there to be extra precautions in terms of public health and safety rather than one leader after the other using fear as a means of controlling the masses. Preying on the gullible or narrow minded as a means of getting their way. As a writer, it is a great setting for a dystopian universe where a group of leaders do the same thing. There have been several thesis statements where many stories held some political backing and have even been brought up in creative writing and political discussion.

But that's the kicker.

When you already live in a dystopian society, where what used to be seen as fiction is now cause for a sick and twisted biography or chapter in a history textbook, what is the point in seeking dystopia between the pages?

My dear reader, are you looking for an escape? Would you rather some sort of alleviation or reprisal where the hero whisks the damsel away from their bindings or stops the villain? Are you looking for a villain with some troubled past that you can easily relate to who just wants to burn the world to little more than a pile of ash and bone?

If so, you have my empathy.

I have written characters like this and I have even gone as far as to sleep away half of the month of November just by writing a story that I could not find upon an old bookshelf in some hole in the wall of a used bookstore.

Even if the cat was the friendliest employee in the shop.

My point to writing this is, it's okay to find escape when the world is crumbling into nothing. It's okay to create your own escape and fall in love with fictional characters who you can trust will never hurt you. After this year, it's easy to say that an escape is perfectly rational.

An Interview with Eliza Loeb

When did you start writing and why?

I started writing when I was very young. My grandmother and I would practice my writing and paragraph accumulation by formulating short stories together. We would do this by writing one sentence, then two sentences and so on.

Which authors or books influenced you the most as a writer?

I would have to say Holly Black, Terry Pratchet and Niel Gaiman were major influences in my writing. Especially given that all three have impacted my view of urban fantasy and the use of psychology and how it can be applied to a story and it's characters. I have also grown up with a lot of mythology and classical influences in my life. But the three aforementioned are the ones that stood out most to me throughout my later adolescence.

Which authors or books had the biggest impact on you as a person?

I really couldn't answer that as there are several who have impacted me. I'm just the crabby little shut in who occasionally emerges from the abyss for some snacks and hot chocolate.

Which of your original twelve Prompt stories are you most pleased with?

I would have to say "The Escape" and "Call Me Kitten", specifically due to the fact that both deal with difficult topics pertaining to psychological trauma and politics in faulty medical systems. I'm not the type of writer who shies away from the gritty parts of life, in fact, I'm more the opposite.

Which of your original twelve Prompt stories did you find the most difficult to write?

The ones where it was me writing and delved into my psychological states. *Uphill Battle* was the first. But the one that stood out to me in particular was when I spoke about a young man who met a fairy in a meadow...that was after I had lost someone close to me.

What book on writing do you recommend?

There are many books on how to write and how not to write, and to ask me what books on writing would I recommend is like asking me how to make a family chicken soup. Everyone has a different style. No one is the same. So if you are going to write, know which audience it is that you want to cater to, know which genre you feel comfortable in and study the classics. Only refer to books on writing to sharpen your tools. Don't refer to them as a means of learning how to write an international novel.

What advice would you give an unpublished writer?

Take as much time honing and improving your skill as possible. It's okay to write fanfiction on a national platform, as some of the most well renowned classical writers of the Renaissance literally wrote fanfiction for funsies and munsies. Dante's Inferno and Paradise Lost are two of them.

Do you have a "dream project" as a writer? What would it be? Share what you feel comfortable sharing.

I have one for adults and one for Young Adults. And then there is the fanfiction that I keep posting because my creative blocks like to claw into me.

The original twelve Prompt stories were written in 2019. In 2020 we all experienced a global pandemic. Did the pandemic impact your writing? How?

The easiest way I can describe it is that I was pretty much watching anime and talking about my characters while taking notes these past six to eight months. The rest is not necessarily rated E for everyone or T for teen.